LOVE'S
Promise

DEDICATION

I dedicate this book to my son, Alexander whom I waited so many years for to enter my life. You truly are a gift and a joy to have in my life.

Also to my husband who always supports me no matter what I get myself into.

And of course my daughter, Samantha, whom I have had the pleasure to watch grow into a beautiful teenager and who shares my love of reading and writing. Maybe one day I will be reading one of her books and feeling the honor of seeing it dedicated to me (hint, hint.)

LOVE'S
Promise

JOHNSON CITY SAGA

BY: LAURIE CLARK

AuthorHouse™
1663 Liberty Drive
Bloomington, IN 47403
www.authorhouse.com
Phone: 1-800-839-8640

Published by AuthorHouse   09/05/2012

ISBN: 978-1-4772-6140-8 (sc)
ISBN: 978-1-4772-6139-2 (e)

Library of Congress Control Number: 2012914844

CHAPTER 1

The bright spring day started like any other. Stacey Bancroft sat at her dining room table drinking her first cup of coffee for the day. It was a beautiful day, she thought to herself, to bad she didn't have anyone to share it with. Stacey smiled when she thought about her two children, Julie and Evan. It wasn't that she was completely alone; she would always have her children there to boost her spirits and make her stop feeling sorry for herself. They were both a blessing, but they hadn't always been that way. When Stacey first found out she was pregnant with Julie, back 6 years ago, she had been scared. The father, a boy she met on a ski trip during winter break, hadn't wanted anything to do with her or the baby. Stacey had become depressed and lonely. Her best friend had left town before she had a chance to tell her about the baby, and after the first chaotic months, things had started to calm down and fall into place.

Evan was her second unexpected surprise 3 years ago. Stacey had met a man at the local fair that was held every summer in June. He had been what they called a Carney, and she had fallen for his charm and rugged good looks.

They hadn't known each other long before he was arrested on a previous outstanding warrant. Stacey didn't want to know what he was charged with, but when the police had questioned her, they had told her drugs. He hadn't seemed the type to sell or use, he hadn't when he was around her, but who knew what occurred before they met. Now she had Evan, her little son, and she was very happy with him. He looked like his father, all that dark hair and haunting eyes. If it was up to her Evan wouldn't know about his father, and Evan's father wouldn't know about him.

Any minute now she would have to wake up the children and get them ready for school. Julie was in kindergarten and Evan attended a pre-school for a half day, then he went to her parent's house until Stacey finished work at 5. It was a good arrangement for her and the children. The best arrangement was that her apartment was right above her work, Johnson's Real Estate. Her boss, Sterling, was also a good friend. It had been Sterling's father, Seth, who had hired her after she had finished her two years of college in Business Administration. That alone had been a blessing.

Sterling was a great boss. He had dated her best friend Lauren for years, and everyone assumed they would get married, but for some reason Lauren had left town without a word to anyone. Sterling had known about the Stacey's pregnancy and he had come around a few times to see how she was doing.

It was nice to have someone other than her family take an interest in her, even if it was to see if she had any information on Lauren. When Seth had offered her the job as his secretary, Stacey knew she had Sterling to thank for the job.

Sighing, Stacey stood up and went to wake up the children. It was days like this that having a man to share the responsibilities with would make her life complete. She was still happy that Lauren had come back to town and that everything had been resolved between them. Lauren and Sterling were engaged and planning a fall wedding, just in time for the arrival of their baby. It had been a shock to them all when Lauren had found out that she was pregnant with Sterling's baby. A good shock that made their getting back together even more important.

This weekend was the engagement party that Seth was throwing them at the Country Club. Stacey hadn't been there before, but she knew that a new dress and shoes were in order. Lauren had asked her to go shopping after work tonight, something Stacey normally didn't cherish, but Lauren had said they would have fun, so she had agreed to go.

The children woke up to her gentle kisses and soft words with no problem and she got them both dressed and driven to school on time. They ate their breakfast at the school, part of the early program that the school had instituted a few years ago. Stacey really liked it, and it fit well with her early mornings. Driving back to the office, Stacey spotted a man walking down the street who looked vaguely familiar. His hair was dark brown, and worn to his shoulders. He had a solid frame that was dressed in a light blue jacket and pair of tight jeans that showed off his excellently shaped ass. Stacey grinned as she drove by and honked her horn in appreciation of the view. When she glanced back in her rearview mirror she saw that the man had stopped and was looking at her car with a frown. Chuckling to herself she continued down the road with a smile on her face.

Once she reached the house, she drove the car in back to her garage, and walked through the backdoor. Stacey started some fresh coffee, and sat behind her desk to boot up her computer for the day. It was almost 8:30 before Sterling made his appearance. He was wearing his usual grin and had a box of donuts under his arm. With a sweeping gesture he placed them on her desk and said "Good Morning" before walking back to his office.

Stacey stared at the donuts with carnal pleasure. It was her biggest downfall in life: sweets. No matter how she tried to avoid them, it was basically impossible. When she finally flipped open the box she let out a groan of despair. There in front of her were two chocolate glazed, a raspberry jelly filled, and two lady fingers. She noticed one was missing, but knew it had to have been the other jelly, Sterling's favorite. Picking up the chocolate glazed she took a bite and let the chocolaty sweetness wash through her system. It was so good to have chocolate in the morning.

Not wanting to eat the whole box, she resolutely closed the lid and placed the box on the counter behind her desk. It would be a long day if all she ate were donuts. She had to remember that tonight she had to try on new dresses, and gaining 10lbs before the fact wouldn't make her feel any better about herself. Quietly humming to herself, Stacey finished her reports and went over the final drafts before sending them onto Sterling.

Sterling came out of the office a few minutes later with the paper reports in his hand. He had grin on his face again, not that he had been without it since Lauren had come back home. If anything, it gave his handsome features an even more rugged appeal.

"These reports are wonderful. If business keeps up we can afford to hire another partner."

"Do you have anyone in mind?" Stacey asked with a smirk.

"Actually I do, but I don't want to put the cart before the horse, so I will just wait and see how things go."

"I'm sure she wouldn't object to joining forces with you. After all, you will be married soon. It would only make sense if Lauren joined Johnson Real Estate."

"To you and me it would make sense, I don't even want to begin to say how Lauren would take it. I'm not willing to risk another argument at this point."

Stacey looked up with a knowing grin. Lauren was opinionated and independent; convincing her to close her new business would probably just cause her to rebel, as Sterling said. She had to hand it to him, he was patient. Most men would insist on an immediate joining, but Sterling always took Lauren's thoughts and feelings into consideration first.

"Well maybe she will see how sensible it will be and decide to make the move on her own."

"My thought precisely. A little hint here, a little nudge there, it makes all the difference."

"Are you meeting with the contractors again today?"

"Actually I have to leave at 11 for a doctor's appointment. It's Lauren's 3 month exam and they are going to do an ultrasound."

"Of course, that's fine. I'll just tell everyone you're out of the office until later."

"Great. Well I have to make some calls and I will see you before I leave."

"Ok." Stacey said going back to the computer and finishing some print outs.

Sterling left a few hours later, and Stacey had the next few hours to relax and make some calls. Sterling didn't mind if she made personal calls during work, he was all about family coming first. She checked on her son and made sure her mom was willing to watch the kids until after her shopping trip with Laurie. She hadn't told Lauren, but she wasn't dragging them with her to look for dresses. It was going to be a relaxing time for them both, just the girls.

At lunch time she closed the office and went around the corner to Julie's Restaurant. It was her favorite place to eat, and they always knew what she wanted to have. She took a seat in the back and waited for her food. The usual crowd had gathered with a few tourists in the mix. Her food arrived and she glanced down to pick up her fork. The bell on the door rang indicating a new customer. Stacey didn't glance up until her mouth was filled with the Goulash that smelled wonderful. She nearly choked on a noodle when she glanced up to see the man with the nice ass standing in front of her.

Reaching for her water, she quickly washed down the rest of the food and wiped her mouth with the napkin. The man was glowering at her with menacing green eyes. She vaguely thought of them as familiar, but again couldn't place him. She wondered why he was staring at her with such contempt, and did her best to keep her face passive.

"Can I help you?" Stacey asked innocently.

"I don't know. I was going to ask you the same thing." He replied gruffly.

"Excuse me?" Stacey asked sweetly.

"Do you go around honking your horn at all strangers, or just strange men?" He asked taking a set across from her.

"I really don't see why that is any of your business. How do you know I was honking at you? I could have been honking at the house you were walking by."

"I wasn't sure, until you just confirmed it. Now I have to ask why?"

"To be honest I don't know." Stacey began with a bit of a smile. "I saw you walking down the street, got a little spunk that told me to do it, and next thing I know, my hand was hitting the horn, and you were giving me a very unhappy scowl. Sorry if it upset you. I would think you would be flattered."

Leaning back in his chair, Robert looked at the woman across the table. His first thought was that she was older than him, probably by about 5 years. His second thought was that she was cute. Her hair was an unruly streaked blond with red flecks that shown in the overhead lights. She had blue eyes that held a hint of mischief twinkling in their depths. Her face was smooth porcelain and she had a dusting of freckles across the bridge of her nose. He couldn't really tell how tall she was since she was sitting down, but her figure was voluptuous.

It took her a minute to realize he was sizing her up, but once she did, Stacey decided to take an inventory of her own. Apart from the dark hair and emerald eyes, he was tall, well built without being over-muscled, he had a nice face with sharp bones but a growth of stubble across his chin. Unlike most men she dated, he didn't have any appearance of tattoos or body piercing, which was probably a good thing.

quiet place. When you have children quiet dinners out is a luxury. Looking over the menu, Stacey almost choked when she saw the prices. She might be able to afford a salad and a glass of water, but that was her limit.

Sensing Stacey distress Lauren said "Don't worry about the price, Sterling is treating tonight. He insisted."

Stacey looked up over the candle that was glowing in the center of their table and met Lauren's stare. She debated whether she should say anything, but not wanting to offend Lauren or Sterling, Stacey gave in gracefully and went about choosing what she wanted.

"I'll have the prime rib with a side salad, baked potato, and a side of sour cream. Maybe I'll be daring and try a Strawberry Daiquiri for a drink." Stacey ordered when the waiter came around.

"And I'll have the barbequed chicken with the rice and corn. Just a glass of water for me to drink please." Lauren ordered.

When the waiter left Stacey glanced at Lauren and grinned. "You haven't changed; you were always going for the cheapest thing on the menu."

"I can't help it. Sterling is trying to break me, but I just can't help myself. Anyway, it wasn't the cheapest. I think the Fish was a dollar cheaper." Lauren laughed.

"So what type of dress are you thinking about?" Stacey asked sipping her Daiquiri when it arrived.

"For the wedding or the party?" Lauren countered sipping her water.

"Either" Stacey replied

"Well for the party something summery. Maybe a flowing pink or blue concoction with flowers and lace. I don't know whatever I see that catches my eye. For the wedding, I have definite plans. It has to be long and elegant. I want poof. Even if I have a burgeoning waistline, I want to look fabulous. I don't plan on doing this again, and I want to do it right."

"Good choice. Make Sterling realize he got the right girl, finally." Stacey replied.

The food arrived and Stacey started to salivate just thinking about the taste of that steak. Lauren gasped at the size of her chicken. They started eating right away. A lot of ohhs and ahhs were heard from them both. It was wonderful. They continued talking as they ate mouthfuls of food.

After dinner, they walked to the boutiques on the top floor of the mall. Stacey held her belly and groaned as she pictured herself trying to squeeze into a dress. Maybe dessert hadn't been such a good idea, but that chocolate torte was just too much to resist.

Lauren went to one rack while Stacey went to another. Soon Stacey discovered she had 5 potential outfits in her arms. Looking over at Lauren she saw that Lauren was equally leaden with clothing. They laughed at each other and headed to the dressing room. The first two outfits Stacey tried on were not anything to talk about. Maybe 10 years ago she could have pulled them off, but not now. Her hips were a lot wider after giving birth to two children, and her breasts had developed significantly. The next outfit was better, but not what she was looking for. The last two were equally ok, but not quite "it".

Lauren came out wearing a flowing emerald green gown. With Lauren's blonde hair and light complexion rosy with her pregnancy, the gown made her look breath taking. Stacey gasped and smiled. That dress was definitely a keeper.

"You look amazing." Stacey breathed as she walked towards Lauren.

"You think so?" Lauren asked looking at herself in the mirror with a frown.

"It's perfect. The color goes so well with your complexion. Sterling will die when he sees you in this dress."

"Then I guess my job here is almost done." Lauren laughed as she walked back into the dressing room to change.

Stacey walked back to the racks to find something else that might catch her eye. After looking through everything, she gave up. Nothing was close to what she wanted. Sighing with dejection, she turned towards the register where Lauren was checking out. As her eyes scanned by the register, she did a double take as her eyes landed on a dress on the discount rack. From across the room it was just another piece of fabric, but the color was so bright it just caught her eye. Walking quickly, as if in a dream, Stacey crossed the room. She threw aside some other dresses, and yanked the dress off the rack. This was the dress, she thought to herself with delight.

Walking to the dressing room, her eyes focused, she didn't notice Lauren's frown as she ignored her calling her name. Pealing her clothing off, Stacey stepped into the hot pink number and pulled the zipper up the back. It fit as if it was made for her body. Usually she wasn't one to wear such a bright color, but this dress was the exception. It was as if it was designed by someone who had her in mind. It was an off the shoulder number with a neckline that almost bordered on scandalous. It would have to be worn without a bra, but she didn't care. It was snug through the waist, which emphasized her incredible figure. It flared just past the waist through her hips, her problem area. It fell into a beautiful tier of ruffles to her knees. Add a pair of black silk stockings and some killer black stilettos and she was set.

She walked out of the dressing room and Lauren gasped. Her hand flew to her mouth and her eyes widened. She took in the full picture standing in front of her and a wide, mischievous smile curved her lips. *This was the dress,* Lauren thought to herself. It had "Stacey" written all over it.

"Oh my God, it's perfect." Lauren said walking to Stacey.

"I know. I can't believe I almost never saw it. It was fate. I don't care how much it costs, this is the dress."

"Definitely." Lauren breathed.

Stacey changed back out of the dress and walked to the counter ready to get sick. It didn't matter if it was more than her yearly salary, she had to own it. Getting ready to reach for the plastic, she almost sank through the floor with relief when she amount came up on the register.

"With the discount it is $149.99." The saleswoman said.

Stacey pulled out the cash she had been saving and when her sale was complete gripped the dress bag to her as they walked out of the store.

"Where to now?" Lauren asked looking down the hallway.

"I think the shoes are next." Stacey said feeling giddy.

Shoes were actually easy. Lauren grabbed a pair of ½ inch strappy sandals in a sedate silver color, and Stacey found her 3 inch stilettos in black with diamond studs. The shopping trip had been a success, and they went home with smiles on their faces.

Robert at that time was at Sterling's house having a few beers. He had surprised Sterling with an invitation for pizza and beer after work. Since Lauren was out on a shopping trip for the party Saturday, Sterling was more than happy to talk to his brother for a while. The evening had gone well. They had talked about the wedding, and as Robert was best man he had discussed some of the details with Sterling about the bachelor party. Now it was about 8 and Sterling was pretty mellow after his 4th beer. Working up the courage to ask his question, Robert figured now was the time.

"So, I hear you have a woman named Stacey working for you." Robert said none too subtly.

"Yeah, she's been there about 4 years now. Dad hired her as a favor to me. She's a friend of Laurens." Sterling replied casually.

"I see. I don't think I've met her have I?" Robert asked looking out over the backyard.

"I don't think so. You were away when she came to work for Dad, and since you just got back a year ago and you haven't made your way over to my office to see me, I'd figure that you probably never ran into her."

"I guess that would make it difficult to have met her than." Robert said finishing his beer.

"Yeah it would. So why the sudden interest?"

"I happened to have run into Stacey today at Julie's and was surprised when the waitress said she worked for my own brother. She's kind of cute."

"The waitress?" Sterling asked trying to goad his brother.

"Stacey!" Robert said exasperated.

"Oh, yeah I guess. She has two kids you know." Sterling said matter-of-factly.

"No, I didn't know. She married?"

"Nope, two different daddies, none of which decided to stick around. She's had a tough time with men. She deserves a lot better than the losers she usually dates."

"Hum." Robert said nonchalantly looking back at his beer bottle.

"If you are thinking of a quick one night stand, think elsewhere. She doesn't need any more trouble. Besides Lauren would kill you if you ruined her wedding. Stacey is her maid of honor."

"I'm not thinking of anything." Robert said defensively, "Just asking a question."

"Sure." Sterling said.

"It's true. I just met her anyway. She honked her horn at me and I made a big stink about it. She got mad and left me sitting there as she stalked out the door. Real fireball if you ask me."

"That's Stacey. Always the risk taker. She is trying to put her life together for the kids. I just think sometimes she misses the carefree days. Who wouldn't? I'm sure after the baby is born Lauren and I will feel the same way. Unlike Stacey, however, we have each other, she doesn't have anyone. That's why I helped her get the job and the apartment."

"You're a good man Sterling. Maybe I should take a page out of your book?"

"Don't be a smart ass. I'm not perfect. You know what happened with me and Lauren?" Sterling asked and then when Robert shook his head Sterling continued, "Well it was Stacey who I almost betrayed her with. That's another reason I helped her get the job. I felt bad about what happened."

"No way!" Robert exclaimed at hearing that bit of news.

"Yeah, all these years of blaming Lauren and it was me and Stacey who caused her to bolt. I guess I never went into much detail with you about what happened, but apparently Lauren had come to the park after I had gotten there. I saw Stacey lying in our spot wearing Lauren's dress and I assumed it was Lauren. Things got pretty hot and heavy; let's just say if I hadn't said my nickname for Lauren, Stacey wouldn't have stopped me. I'm just damn glad I did. Lauren saw us together, thought we were double crossing her, and ran. That was the night she was going to tell me about the baby, the same night I was going to propose."

"Wow that sounded messy. But you and Stacey didn't actually have sex, right?" Robert asked cautiously.

"No we didn't. Like I said she stopped me just in time. It was a lucky break. Let me tell you, I don't assume anything anymore. If it's dark, I make sure and ask who I'm with before jumping the gun."

"Good advice. I'll remember that to." Robert said with a laugh. In his mind he couldn't believe anyone could confuse Lauren and Stacey, but he didn't know them back in school, so maybe they were more alike than now.

"Well I guess I should be going. Lauren should be back soon and I don't want to interrupt any pre-wedding talk. I'll see you Saturday at the Country Club."

"Alright and thanks for coming over tonight. I miss these brotherly talks." Sterling laughed as Robert walked to his car.

Sterling watched Robert drive away in a quick flash of red paint and shiny chrome. *Some things never changed* he thought to himself. Robert's visit had been a surprise. They hadn't really gotten close since Robert came home from college. Partly it was his fault, Sterling chastised himself. He had been so busy working, than when Lauren showed up everything went crazy. Well hopefully things would calm down and he could start to develop a relationship with Robert. They had been close years ago, before Sterling had gone away to boarding school. Robert, 5 years younger had idolized his older brother. When Sterling had come back to town and moved in with his father Robert had been a cocky teenager. Sterling had enjoyed watching his brother grow up before he was sent away, but after he came home Robert didn't want anything to do with him. Sterling had tried to help him with his school and social life, but Robert had nixed that idea quickly. Lauren had been the center of his attention for many of those years. After she had left, he had become withdrawn and devoted to work. Maybe he should have tried to stay connected with Robert, but by then Robert had taken an interest in the stage. He had graduated from school and moved to California where he had tried to make it big for the last 3 years.

He was a little puzzled by the questions about Stacey. They had come out of the blue. Sterling hadn't known what to say. Had Robert taken an interest in Stacey? Was it just physical? Sterling didn't know, but he hoped that Robert would take his advice and stay away, at least until after the wedding. Lauren would be mad if something happened to ruin the wedding. With those swinging hormones he didn't want to be in the fray.

He saw a car round the corner and slow at his driveway. It was Lauren's car. With a grin on his face he walked over to meet her as she got out. Her face was radiant and she pulled out a few bags to hand to him. Reaching over, Sterling grabbed her in his arms and gave her a deep kiss.

"What was that for?" Lauren asked breathlessly as he pulled away.

"Just wanted you to know I love you." Sterling replied.

"Of course I know silly. I love you too."

Feeling like a million bucks, Sterling swept Lauren and all her purchases up into his arms and carried her into the house. As long as she was with him, everything else would work out fine, he thought to himself kicking the door closed and walking up the stairs.

CHAPTER 3

To Stacey, the rest of the week passed by quickly. Saturday morning dawned sunny and warm. The children were going to spend the day with her parents out of town. They were taking them to a zoo that was about an hour away. They had decided to spend the whole day and come back tomorrow morning. Stacey figured that was a great idea. It gave her plenty of time to get ready for the party, and time to relax when she got home. She could spend as long as she wanted at the Country Club, and not have to worry about picking the kids up before their bedtime.

Stacey had packed their things the night before, and her parents were coming by around noon to pick them up. Stacey couldn't wait. A whole afternoon to pamper herself. It was really almost too much for her to comprehend, almost. At 11:30 she fed the children a light lunch. Her parents said they would take them to McDonald's, but she didn't want them to be hungry in the car. At noon her parents arrived as promised. Stacey was biting her nails with worry that something would happen to cancel the trip. Her parents assured her that all was well, and after a lot of kisses and hugs the children were bundled out the door and driving down the street.

The apartment was silent. Stacey let out a sigh of relief then leaned against the closed door and staring around her. *What to do first?* She thought to herself. A facial, a manicure, a shower, maybe just pick up the house and then get ready. Quickly she scrubbed down the surfaces of the table, counter, and the sink. Dishes were thrown in the dishwasher and started. She started some laundry, made the children's beds, changed the sheets on her own bed and made it, vacuumed the floors, and finally at 3 o'clock she jumped into the shower. She didn't want to take the time to do a bath because she still had her hair and nails to do before leaving.

By 5:30 Stacey was dressed and ready to go. The dress was as beautiful as it had been in the store. When she had first taken it out of the bag, she had stared at the bright color and prayed that she hadn't imagined how gorgeous she had looked in it at the store earlier in the week. Now with her make-up done, hair piled loosely on top of her head, nails painted a matching pink, panty hose and stilettos, she had to admit she looked fabulous.

Grabbing her little black purse Stacey locked the door and went out the back to the garage. As she sat behind the wheel, she took a deep breath. This was it. It was the chance of a life time. She was going to have a good time and forget for just one night she was a single mother of two children. Tonight was her night.

With that thought in mind, Stacey cranked up the music and zoomed down the street. The Country Club was on the outside of town. The road had recently been paved, and the view from the top of the hill was breathtaking. Stacey pulled up to the front door, and a valet took her keys from her hand. Never having experienced valet parking, she wasn't sure what to do. He gave her a ticket and told her to just go inside. A little unsure of herself, Stacey stared at the door until she heard a voice behind her.

"Well, well, well we met again." A familiar voice said mockingly.

Stacey turned around and came face to face with the mocking green eyes of the man she had so stupidly honked at the other day. She groaned as she looked at his black tuxedo. He looked wonderful. His once shoulder length hair was now cut to just about his ears. It was slicked back with mousse and it made him look even more handsome than she remembered. The cut of the tuxedo showed off his impressive build, and she had a chance to see some nice pecks when he walked towards her.

"What are you doing here?" Stacey asked in a whisper.

"I'm a guest." Robert said casually looking her up and down.

She looked incredible. Her hair was piled on top of her head in such a way that made him want to run his hands through it so that it hung down around her shoulders. Her dress was killer. It was hot pink and tight. He almost had a heart attack when she'd turned around to face him. He imagined running his hand down the plunging line of her dress and pushing it aside to view those tempting breasts. Her legs were incased in black silk, and with those heels they seemed to go on for miles. Images on them wrapped around him teased his mind.

"Guest?" Stacey asked confused.

"Is that so difficult to believe?" Robert asked taking her arm as she stared dumbly at him and walking them through the door.

"I don't know, I guess I'm just surprised to see you here."

They entered the club and he led her to the room towards the back of the building. Stacey could feel the heat of his hand through the back of her dress. His leg brushed hers as they walked side by side to the entryway of the banquet room. Casting him a covert look under her eyelashes, Stacey had to admit he was sexy. At the closed doorway, he stopped and turned towards her. Dropping his hand from around her back, he gently picked up her hand and brought it to his lips. The kiss was light and seductive. Stacey felt a tingle go through her body. The same tingle she had felt yesterday at the restaurant.

"I'll see you later." He replied softly and letting go of her hand he bowed and walked back the way they had just come.

Stacey watched as he left the building. She was holding her hand cradled against her body. Looking down at it, she frowned and then shook herself. Was she crazy? She didn't even know his name. When he had kissed her hand she had thought about all the other places she wanted him to kiss her. Her checks flushed at her thoughts and she turned and opened the door.

The room was decorated in green and gold. Balloons were on the tables and hanging from the ceiling. It was supposed to be a family and close friend's affair, but judging by all the tables, they expected at least 100 people. No wonder that man had been invited. It looked like half the town would be there. Stacey glanced around the room looking for Lauren or Sterling. She didn't see them, but spotted Seth at the bar. Walking across the room she went up to him and tapped him on the shoulder.

Turning Seth's eyes bugged out of his head when he saw her, "Mother of God, Stacey, you look fabulous."

"Thank you Seth." Stacey replied as they embraced.

"Where are Lauren and Sterling?" She asked looking around again.

"Not here yet. I figured they'd be late. Those two can't keep their hands off each other for 5 minutes." Seth grumbled good naturedly.

"Well you must remember how it was being in love and all."

"I guess." He grumbled some more while handing her a drink.

Sipping the white wine, Stacey continued to look around the room. *Where was that guy? Maybe Seth could tell me who he is if I point him out,* she thought to herself. She couldn't see him anywhere and she wondered if maybe he had lied and wasn't a guest at all, but worked at the club. The band soon started to play, and Lauren and Sterling arrived amidst a lot of cheers and shouts. Stacey soon started to dance with a string of people; Seth, Sterling, and John, a friend of Sterling's from boarding school, as well as a few men she knew from the office. She was having a good time, but her thoughts wondered to the mystery man.

Soon they were eating dinner and it was time for a few toasts. Stacey sat next to Lauren and Sterling at a center table. She noticed the chair opposite her was vacant. She turned to Lauren and asked whose seat it was.

"It's for Robert, Sterling's brother. Something came up at the last minute and he said he would be late. He should be here any minute to give his toast."

"Sterling has a brother?" Stacey asked

"Yeah, you might not remember him. He's like 5 years younger than Sterling. Robert looks kind of like Sterling, but not as muscular."

"Oh" was all Stacey could mutter as an uneasy feeling crept up on her. It couldn't be, she said to herself.

Seth gave the first toast. It was filled with tears and laughs. Lauren gave him a kiss when he was finished and thanked him for his kind words about her. Stacey waited as everyone quieted down and wondered if she would be next, or if the infamous Robert would show up. Just then she heard music start in the background and the lights dimmed. Stacey glanced around puzzled, but Lauren laughed and Sterling cursed.

Suddenly actors appeared in the center of the room. A short play was acted out in front of its willing audience. Stacey saw it was a reenactment of Lauren's and Sterling's life together. Stacey was captivated by the show. The actor that placed Sterling was very good, but he wore a mask over his eyes, as he moved around the stage he turned towards her and Stacey's breath caught as her eyes collided with liquid green ones. It was the mystery man. Smiling at the remembrance of her incredulous response to his being a guest, Stacey gave a mock bow to him from her chair. He grinned and continued his performance.

When the play ended Lauren jumped to her feet and gave the man a hug. Sterling slowly stood and went to shake his hand.

Taking the microphone from the actor, Sterling said to the crowd, "Many of you might not recognize this man with the mask, but I would like to introduce you all to Robert, my baby brother."

The man ripped off his mask and took a bow while everyone cheered and clapped. Stacey went still. Robert was Sterling's brother. The mystery man was Robert. Robert glanced over at her again and saw her face go blank. *What was wrong with her?* He wondered. She must have known who he was, hadn't she? The look on her face said no, but maybe she was just shocked at his being here. He would soon find out but now he had to give his toast.

"Thank you everyone. I just wanted to say a quick word about Lauren and my brother Sterling. I am so honored to be the best man at their wedding. Lauren has been a great addition to our family already, and when she finally ties the knot with my older brother, that addition will be even more complete. I hope them nothing but joy and happiness, and wish that someday I can have even half the love they share with someone and I will be a complete man. To Sterling and Lauren."

More clapping ensued and Stacey clapped to. It was a beautiful heartfelt speech, and she could only say that she agreed with Robert. His words mirrored the ones she was about to utter to the crowd.

Lauren motioned for her to come to the center of the room with them and unable to decline as the maid of honor, Stacey went slowly. Robert handed her the microphone as she passed him on her way to Lauren's side. His fingers grazed hers and she felt that spark go up her hand. Clearing her throat Stacey tried to calm her nerves. This was difficult enough on any average day, but today with Robert there, speaking in front of everyone was even harder.

"I just want to more or less say the same thing Robert just said. Lauren and Sterling were made for each other. From the day they met it was fated they would be together. Some strange things have happened in the past that have kept them apart, but now they have found each other again, and I am blessed to be a part of their lives. I hope that someday, I too will be blessed to find a love as special and all consuming as these two have found. I love you both, may you know love and happiness always."

The room clapped and cheered again and Lauren and Sterling hugged her. She started to walk away, but Robert grabbed her hand and swung her around into a dance. The music started and Stacey found she couldn't leave him on the floor, what would people think? They danced the waltz slowly and closely. Robert had his arms around her waist and seemed to be gradually pulling her closer and closer as they went in circles. Stacey tried to stay stiff and keep her distance, but he wasn't letting her. His hands caressed her hips and she slowly began to relax.

By the end of the song Stacey had laid her head on his shoulder, and had wound her arms around his neck. They were barely turning in a circle, just swaying back and forth on the floor. The next song started and they continued to dance. Stacey wasn't really listening to the music anymore, she was just happy to be held and touched by Robert. After a few minutes, however, she realized Robert had stopped moving altogether. She lifted her head to look at him and his eyes were that emerald fire again. She tried to jerk back but his hands tightened on her hips making her fully aware of his manhood, fully aroused against the junction of her thighs.

He leaned down and whispered in her ear, "Let's go for a walk."

Stacey nodded and they quickly walked out the side door towards the gazebo. Robert kept an arm around her shoulders and she had her hand around his waist. They reached the gazebo and found it empty. It was dark out now, and the lights around the outside of the wooden frame made it look romantic. Walking up the steps, Stacey first, they went to the far side and looked over the lake. Robert walked up behind her and placed his hands on her shoulders, caressing them lightly.

Stacey shivered in reaction to his touch. She felt so alive with him by her side. She couldn't remember the last time she felt so alive. It had been years, or maybe never. Julie's father had been a diversion for a winter of boredom. Evan's father had been a temptation for the unknown. Robert was something else altogether.

"Are you cold?" Robert asked feeling her shiver.

"No, I'm fine." Stacey whispered not turning around.

"Do you want to walk by the lake?" He asked stroking his hand down her arm and back up again.

"Sure if you want to." Stacey replied finally turning around.

The look in his eyes said he wanted to do other things with her than walk, but she assumed he was trying to be patient and polite. He grabbed her hand and they walked down the steps and around the side of the gazebo towards the lake. The night was cool, but not cold. The ground, however, was moist and uneven. Her stilettos didn't like the feeling, and she stumbled a few times. Robert looked down and frowned. He tightened his hold on her arm and they walked closer towards the woods where the ground wasn't so unsteady.

"Thanks." Stacey said with a laugh as they finally made their way to the paved walkway.

"No problem. I didn't think about your shoes when I suggested a walk by the lake."

"Me either." Stacey confessed.

Robert stopped walking and since they were holding hands she jerked back when his arm didn't go any further.

"Do you want to know why I didn't think about it?" Robert whispered pulling her towards him.

"Sure, if you want to tell me." Stacey whispered back staring down at the ground.

"I guess it has to do with that dress you're wearing." Robert said looking down at her bent head.

Stacey looked up at him and stared. Was he saying he liked her dress or didn't like her dress? She couldn't tell from his tone. The look in his eyes said he liked it, liked it a lot. The hot green fire of his eyes, the tight lines around his mouth, and the tension in his body all told her he found her dress as sexy and bold as she did. Smiling now that she was surer of herself, Stacey walked up to him and put her hands against his chest, running them over the inside vest poking through the jacket.

"I wore it to assure that I would get lucky tonight." Stacey whispered seductively as her lips feathered across his.

Robert groaned in surrender, a man could only take so much teasing. Stacey was practically offering herself to him and he was only human. Taking her invitation, Robert deepened the kiss as his arms went around her waist and yanked her body to his. As first kisses go, this one was a torrent of emotions. Want, need, fire, desire, give and take, everything rolled into one. Robert moved his hand over her back, around under her arms and up to her breasts. Playing with the plunging neckline he lightly teased the side of her breasts with the slid of his fingernails. Stacey groaned and thrust her tongue into his mouth. His touch was electric and she wanted more. Taking her hint, Robert pushed the filmy fabric aside and cupped her naked breasts in his hands. They were full and filled his palms to perfection. Her nipple went ridged as he caressed it with the pad of his thumb.

Stacey's hands moved from his chest to his neck. She pulled his head down further to deepen the kiss even more. This was what she wanted. The mind numbing feelings that came with sex. It had been over 3 years since she had been with a man, and her body was crying for attention.

"Take me home." Stacey whispered as she pulled his mouth away from hers.

"Are you sure?" Robert asked in a daze of need.

"I'm sure." Stacey replied grabbing his hand and walking quickly to the parking lot.

Half way there her heel hit a rut and she almost went down. Growling with unfulfilled passion, Robert picked her up and carried Stacey the rest of the way. The valet hurriedly got her car and Robert put her in the passenger side and got behind the wheel.

"You know where I live?" Stacey asked breathlessly.

"Yeah, I know where you live." Robert said throatily as he drove a little recklessly down the hill to Faville Street.

He parked in the back and helped her out of the car. Stacey grabbed his hands and led him to the back door. When they reached the door, Robert pulled her back into his arms and kissed her with controlled passion. Stacey barely could unlock the door while her mind whirled. They stumbled up the steps as they kissed and touched through their clothing.

When they got to her apartment door, Robert took her keys and unlocked the door himself. Looking at her, he considered asking her again if she was sure, but Stacey took the keys from him, walked through the door, and pulled him in before shutting and locking it behind him. Robert bent down and lifted her again, carrying her unerringly into her bedroom. Later Stacey wondered how he knew which one was hers, but now she didn't think, she felt.

Robert laid her on her comforter. He took off her heels and his shoes. He chucked his coat, vest, shirt, and cumber bun. Lying down on the bed beside her, he slowly lowered the zipper of her dress. He hooked his fingers into the straps and pulled it down over her breasts, past her waist, over her hips and down her legs. Robert than threw it on the floor and looked back at her. She lay naked except the black lace garter belt, lacey black panties, and silk stockings. Her skin was flawless, white as porcelain and smooth to the touch.

Tracing his finger up her stocking, he traced the path his eyes had taken. He continued to move over her bare thigh, up to her garter belt, over her belly, and up to her breasts. He stopped to cup them in his hands and bent down to suckle at first one than the other. Stacey arched off the bed and grabbed his head, holding him to her. Robert stayed for awhile before tracing his path back down her body. He paid homage to her stomach, where he could see faint marks from the birth of her children. He moved his fingers down to her panties and slipped a finger inside. Her skin was hot and moist. Fighting to control his reaction, Robert started a slow assault on her delicate flesh.

Stacey breathing started to hitch and her hands became restless. Robert was doing things she couldn't remember every having done to her before. No man had ever taken the time to touch or caress her this way before. He kissed her stomach, touched her scars and brought tears of gratitude to her eyes. When his finger found her hot flesh, however, she knew she was in over her head. He touched and teased, slipping his finger in and out of her flesh as she moaned in pleasure. Her hands didn't know what to do with themselves. She wanted to touch him, but he was too far away. Sensing her distress, Robert grabbed her hands with his free hand and moved them to the bedrails. He folded them around the metal frame and seeing her confusion he grinned a sexy grin before moving back down her body.

Stacey soon found out what he was about. Robert slithered down her body, kissing as he went. His head stopped in front of her womanhood. She frowned down at him as he moved her panties to the side trying to get better access. Not liking them in the way, he finally grabbed the material with two hands and ripped it apart. Stacey gasped in shock as her new underwear was torn in two. Her next thought was oh well. Robert parted the folds of her womanhood and fastened his mouth over it. Stacey arched off the bed as she climaxed into his mouth. It was so strong and fast she didn't have time to think about it. Her hands tightened on the bed frame and her legs went around his neck to hold him there. She moaned and cried out in shock and delight as his tongue continued to lick and thrust into her tightening flesh.

After she had settled down a bit, Stacey let go of the rail and pulled his head up. She had never felt anything like that before, but as pleasant as it was, she wanted him with her. Robert sensed her need, and he quickly removed the rest of his clothing. He reached for the condom in his pocket and Stacey grabbed it from him, sheathing his engorged manhood herself. Robert thought he had never seen a sexier sight in his life than Stacey placing the condom on his manhood. She ran her hand down the length of him, and then to his balls. She squeezed and messaged him until he was ready to explode.

Grabbing her hands in his, Robert placed them on either side of her head as he spread her legs and thrust into her. Stacey arched to meet him, and wrapped her stocking clap legs around his waist. Robert didn't think he had felt anything more erotic than making love to a woman naked except for her stockings and garter belt. It was like a fantasy come true.

Stacey reached up with her neck and kissed his lips. She could taste herself on his lips and found it exciting.

She deepened the kiss, and Robert leaned down over her more to follow her mouth. Their tongues mated as their bodies mated. He thrust into her hard and deep, and she arched her hips to meet each thrust of his body. Soon he felt her tighten around him again and he rocked against her without withdrawing, sending her over the peak again. As she clutched his hips with her thighs Robert plunged deep and followed her over.

When his pulse had slowed and he could breathe again, Robert rolled to her side taking Stacey with him. He tucked her head into his shoulder and drew a quilt from the bottom of the bed over their cooling bodies. Stacey laid her hand on his chest and kissed his shoulder. They both sighed and within minutes were asleep.

Robert awoke first. It was still dark out and glancing over at the clock he noticed it was about 2am. Stacey was still pressed against his side, naked except the stocking clad legs, one of which was thrown over his legs. Stroking her back he started to feel himself harden with renewed desire. He couldn't remember wanting a woman as much as he wanted Stacey. He wasn't sure if he liked the feeling.

As he pondered his thoughts, Stacey stretched and rubbed her bare breasts against his side. She was filled with languid feelings of desire and satisfaction for Robert. Now that she that she had been fully satisfied, she wanted to have that feeling again. She knew Robert was awake. She felt him lightly stroking her back, and she felt his sharp intake of breath when she stretched and rubbed against him.

"How about a shower?" Stacey asked propping herself on an elbow to look at his features outlined by the sliver of light coming through the window.

"Sounds good." Robert replied turning to look at her.

Stacey decided to tease him a little before getting up. He seemed so suddenly serious, and she didn't want him to be. Rolling over on top of him she gave him a quick kiss and then rolled to the floor.

"Last one in has to wash the other's back." She called as she started towards the bathroom.

"Not fair." Robert yelled getting off the bed.

Stacey beat him there, mostly because he wasn't sure exactly where the bathroom was. She had the water started and was getting towels out as Robert looked around the room taking in the rose and white theme she had going on. There were toys for the children on the floor near the tub, a little training potty in the corner, and an assortment of children's clothing on the floor near the hamper.

"Don't look at the mess. I was trying to clean before I left, but the house is such a disaster. Two kids can really do that to you."

Stacey looked at him over her shoulder trying to gage his reaction to her words. Did he know she had two children already? Had Sterling told him? What did he think? If he did know, did he think she was easy? So many questions unanswered, yet she didn't want to know the answers tonight. Tonight was her time. No children, no responsibilities, just plain grown-up fun.

Robert looked at her blank face trying to read her thoughts. He knew she was waiting for him to respond to her statement, but he really didn't know what to say. He knew about her kids, of course, but right now he didn't know where this thing between them was going. Should he say something?

Deciding to leave it for another time, if there was one; Robert got in the shower behind her and grabbed the soap. He lathered up the washcloth and started washing her back. Soon his hand was wondering to her stomach, her arms, and her breasts, down to her hips, her legs and then to her womanhood. Stacey leaned against the shower wall to support her weak legs.

Not wanting to be the only one to experience the sensation, Stacey grabbed the washcloth off the rack and lathered it with the soap. She pulled Robert up and leaned him against the wall as she teased him the same way that he had done to her. After the water had started to turn cold, they both got out of the shower and helped each other dry off. When they had finished, they went back to the bedroom and made love again. Stacey thought it was even better than the first time because now that their need had been quenched, they were able to take their time and savor each other. When they had fallen asleep, they both didn't awaken again until morning.

CHAPTER 4

Morning arrived with a clap of thunder and a bolt of lightning. Stacey started out of her dreamless sleep and sat up in bed trying to figure out what was going on. Robert, who was lying on his stomach, threw out an arm and pulled her back to his side. Stacey lay down and remembered the events of last night. It all seemed a fabulous dream, but Robert was still beside her in her bed, naked and incredibly sexy with his rumpled hair and stubble on his chin.

Stacey glanced over at the clock on her bedside table and moaned at the hour. It was already 10, and the kids would be back by 12. She had to get up, eat, and get ready for their return all in two hours. Her biggest problem, however, was lying beside her. What was she to do about him? Last night had been fabulous. She couldn't remember a night where she had had such energy and passion. Today she felt like a new woman, ready to face the world, and all on a max of 5 hours sleep.

Robert peaked at Stacey through a half opened eye. She had a frown between her eyebrows and her lips were set in a sweet little pucker of confusion. He wanted to reach over and kiss that frown away. Last night had been incredible. She was incredible. Her innocent charm and passion had been an effective aphrodisiac that continued to arouse his need for her.

"Good morning." He murmured huskily turning fully towards her and giving her a kiss on the forehead.

Stacey turned and offered a slight smile, "Good morning to you."

"Are you hungry? We can go around the corner to Julie's if you want."

"Um, actually I don't have time. My kids will be back soon. I think a quick breakfast would be best."

"Ok. I'll make it, you get dressed. What do you want?"

He was an economy of motion. Robert had rolled off the bed and was already partially dressed before she realized what had happened. Stacey stared at him in confusion.

"You're going to make breakfast for me?" She said incredulously.

"What, no one ever made you breakfast after a night of mind blowing sex before?"

Stacey didn't like the note of surprise in his tone. It implied that she was missing something. She just shrugged her shoulders and stared at him. Robert took pity on her and gave her a cocky grin.

"It's the least I can do for you. We had a great night together, you deserve some special attention."

Leaning over he took her lips in a hungry kiss that left her speechless. She wrapped her arms around his neck and pulled him towards her. He purposely kept his distance, and released her lips.

"No more of that for now. Get dressed. I'll make breakfast and coffee."

With that he turned and went to the kitchen. Stacey touched her throbbing lips and sighed. Would there be a next time? Not wanting to ruin the rest of her morning, she did as he directed and got dressed. By the time she was dressed and presentable, Robert had made French toast, coffee, and some scrambled eggs. Stacey's stomach rumbled from the wonderful smells permeating the apartment.

"Wow, you are great." She said in awe of his handy work.

"Well I'll just have to take you word for it." He replied sassily with a wink that made her blush at her unintentional double entrée.

They ate in silence. Both had worked up an appetite after last night's activities. Robert even helped her load the dishwasher and clean up the kitchen. By the time they had finished it was 11:30. Robert knew she was worried about his being there when the kids returned so he hastily gathered the rest of his clothing and got ready to leave.

"Well I guess I'll be going. I really had a good time."

"Me too, thanks for breakfast. No one has made me breakfast since I was a kid."

Robert found that statement sad and unacceptable. Stacey deserved someone to pamper her and her kids. He just wasn't sure he was the one who could do it. He didn't even have a job. What could he, an unemployed actor, provide for her and her children? Depressed at the thought he walked to the door.

"Let me walk you out." Stacey said starting to walk with him.

"No!" Robert said hurriedly, "I want to remember you here, in your apartment."

"You sound like we will never see each other again." Stacey said unevenly.

"I guess that's up to you." Robert said looking at her face, "I don't have anything to offer you Stacey. I don't even have a job."

Stacey laughed. Was he kidding? He had just offered her everything last night, mindless pleasure and then breakfast the next morning? Who could ask for more?

"I'm not looking for a husband or a father for my children. I'm looking for a companion, someone who wants to be with me, for me. I don't need or want your money. I work and take care of my family. It has taken me years to get there, but I have finally accomplished complete security. If you think you can be those things that I am looking for, than you let me know."

Robert looked at her and couldn't believe her candor. He had never met anyone that had actually spelled out the terms of a relationship, and demanded so little. She didn't want love, marriage, money, or any of the factors most women hounded him for. It was like a dream come true, but for some reason the dream seemed empty to him now. With Stacey he actually didn't find those things appealing.

"Can I give you an answer now, or do I have to wait?" Robert asked walking back across the room towards her.

"Now is fine." Stacey whispered as he stepped in front of her.

"I want to be with you. Whether it is for a week, a month, a year, or whatever you want to give me. I want to be with you. The question is do you want to be with me?"

In response Stacey reached up and brought his lips to hers. The kiss was deep, filled with unfulfilled hunger and need. It conveyed her desire to have him with her. Robert returned the kiss with equal hunger. This was what they would start with, he promised, but it would be more, much, much more.

He broke the kiss first, laying his check against hers and he caressed her back. Taking a steadying breath he stepped back and smiled at her tenderly.

"I'll be in touch." Robert said, and then he was gone.

Stacey slumped against the couch she was leaning against. What had happened? She wondered to herself.

She had just proposed an agreement with a man she hardly knew, other than he was Sterling's brother, and a stallion in the sack. She had basically set up a relationship based on sex, not love. It was so unlike her, against everything she had promised to never do again.

Ten minutes later her thoughts were halted as her parents brought her children home. They were excited and full of energy. It had been a great break away for all of them, now life was back to normal, or as normal as she could picture it being. How was she going to cope with a man now that the children were back? She would have to wait and see.

Robert walked home in a good mood, whistling and smiling as he took the long route from Stacey's apartment to his father's house. It was still dark and cloudy, but the rain was holding off. He didn't care if he got caught in it or not, nothing could dampen his spirits. His father was in his study/bedroom working on some business when he arrived home. The nurse that helped take care of his dad after his stroke was in the kitchen making lunch. Robert walked by them all without a word and went to his room. With a quick shower and some fresh clothes he would feel even better.

Robert's plans changed quickly when he found Sterling sitting on his bed legs crossed and arms folded. He knew what this was about, but pretended indifference as he made his journey to the bathroom.

"Don't think you can walk away from me without an explanation." Sterling growled.

Robert raised an eyebrow at him. "I'm not ignoring you or refusing an explanation. I'm taking a shower and changing out of my tux first." Robert said shutting the bathroom door.

Fifteen minutes later Robert emerged in a fresh pair of jeans and a t-shirt. Sterling had been pacing his brother's room trying to think of a tactful way to warn Robert, yet again, to stay away from Stacey. He couldn't really find anything. He really didn't want to be here anyway, it had been at Lauren's insistence that he came.

"So what brings you by big brother?" Robert asked sarcastically rubbing his wet hair with a towel.

"I thought I told you to stay away from Stacey? Do you not understand what those words mean?"

"Oh I heard you loud and clear, the problem is that I don't take orders from you." Robert replied walking to his dresser for some socks.

Sterling growled at his reply. It wasn't anymore than he had expected. What could he do to get Robert to understand his position?

"Lauren is upset. She is worried that something will happen to cause problems."

"Lauren shouldn't worry about something that isn't her business." Robert said sitting on his bed to put on his socks.

"She's pregnant; everything worries her, especially when it comes to the wedding." Sterling sighed sitting down next to Robert.

"So you are here to assure her that nothing will ruin the wedding? You can go back and tell her all is well. Nothing bad will happen. Stacey and I have a mutual arrangement. Actually she was the one that wanted to continue seeing me."

Sterling glanced at Robert and raised an eyebrow. It was his turn to be incredulous. "Really?" Sterling replied hopefully.

"Yeah really. I was willing to back off and keep it at a one night thing, but she said she wanted to see me again.

Actually she wants to keep it basically a physical deal from what I gather. How can any man pass that up? I'm not a saint. She was the one to come on to me yesterday. I told her I didn't think it was a good idea, but she told me to take her to her place. I'm human Sterling, and she looked hot."

Sterling nodded in agreement. Stacey had looked good yesterday. If he wasn't so in love with Lauren he might have taken things to another level with Stacey himself. Add to Robert's confession that she had taken the lead, how could a man turn that down?

"Ok, I'll tell Lauren it's cool between you two, but if something happens in the next few months, you are the number one target, got that?"

"Whatever. I'll take the heat, but don't tell Lauren what I said."

"Believe me, I'm not telling her that her friend is hot for you. That could cause whole other problems I don't want to deal with."

"Ok, can you leave me so I can get some rest now? I didn't get much sleep last night."

"Alright, stop rubbing it in. I get it; you had incredible sex all night last night. Let us older guys have our dignity."

"Don't try to deny that you and Lauren still have all niters. I've seen the way you two look some mornings after a night together."

"Hey, I'm not saying anything. Get some sleep. I'll see you later for dinner."

"Ok, tell Lauren hi for me."

"Will do."

Sterling left and Robert lay down on the bed. He tried to get comfortable, but his thoughts kept drifting to Stacey. He never felt this type of connection with someone he just met before. It was like they knew each other's thoughts. Maybe he was just kidding himself. It wasn't like they had talked much last night. Maybe they had nothing in common other than the incredible chemistry. That alone, in his mind, was enough to keep seeing her. He couldn't imagine not spending at least another night or two with her, just to make sure last night wasn't a fluke.

Turning over he stared out the window and thought about when he would see her again. They hadn't set a date or anything, he just had told her he would be in touch. How lame was that? He sighed disgustingly to himself. She probably figured he would never call and that he had been just running a line. Tomorrow he would make sure Stacey knew how serious he was. With that thought in his head, Robert drifted off to sleep.

CHAPTER 5

When Stacey got to work Monday morning she was so glad the weekend was over. Sunday had turned out to be a nightmare. After her parents had dropped off Julie and Evan, they had eaten lunch together and talked about the kid's trip to the Zoo. After lunch Evan has started to become whiny and unmanageable. She had tried to get him to lay down for his afternoon nap, but to no avail. Julie had than become demanding and clingy. The rest of the night had been a chaotic mess of screaming, whining, tantrums that had resulted in Stacey getting a headache. The kids had gone to bed at 7 and she had joined them shortly after that.

The morning had been hectic because no one had gotten their things out for school the night before. She had had to run around searching for Julie's homework assignment they had finished together Friday night. Evan had decided this morning he wanted to eat before school, and that had set her behind another 15 minutes. It was now ten after 8 and the office wasn't open yet. She pulled into the driveway and noticed a red sports car sitting out front. She didn't recognize it as one of their current clients, so she quickly went through the back and started opening the office.

At 8:30 she had the computers up and running and the coffee made. Going to the front door she flipped the lock and the open sign and sat back down. A minute later, Robert walked in the door.

"Good morning, running behind today?" He asked politely.

"Yeah, it was a bad morning." Stacey mumbled looking at the bouquet of roses in his hand.

"Sorry to hear that, I hope these brighten your day a bit." He said as he handed the flowers to her.

"Thank you." She said sniffing the colored buds with appreciation.

She hadn't ever received flowers for a man before. Well she had from Sterling on her birthday every year, but he was her boss and figured that didn't count.

"I was thinking Sunday about how we left things so up in the air, and I wanted to make sure you knew that I really did want to see you again." He said looking around the office.

"Oh. I guess I hadn't really thought about it. Sunday was so crazy after the kids got home. Thank you though. It was nice of you to come by. Do you want a cup of coffee? I just made it."

"Sure that would be nice. Why don't I get it for you? Tell me how you like it."

Stacey glanced up quickly at his face. Was he playing with her again? She thought to herself. She wasn't used to people being so unreadable, but with Robert she didn't know when he was joking or being serious.

"I like my coffee light with two sugars." Stacey said cautiously

"Ok one light with sugar coming up." Robert said walking to the kitchen.

He returned in minutes with two steaming mugs. Stacey drank hers greedily. Robert sipped his slowly looking at her over his cup as he sipped. Stacey squirmed at his probing stare. *What did he want?* She thought to herself. *Should I be doing or saying something? Oh I hate this.*

"What's wrong?" She finally asked after a few minutes of his continuous gaze.

"Nothing. I was just thinking how beautiful you look." Robert whispered huskily.

Stacey blushed at his candor. No one had ever called her beautiful before. Did he really think that or did he think he had to say it because of Saturday night?

"I'm hardly considered beautiful by any standards." She replied dropping her gaze to the coffee cup in her hands.

"You're wrong." Robert said reaching across the desk to grab her hand. "You are beautiful to me."

He brought her hand to his lips and pressed a light kiss on it before folding his fingers through hers and caressing it with his thumb. Stacey's breath caught in her throat at his touch. He was doing it again, she thought to herself. He was causing that electric feeling to go through her system at his touch.

"I think you're beautiful." Stacey replied blushing again.

Robert grinned and Stacey watched the dimples appear on his cheeks. He looked so young and boyish at that moment. How could anybody resist him when he put on the charm? Was it natural or practiced? Either way she was going to have to be careful not to open her heart to him. He was dangerous, in more ways than one.

"Well I have to get back to work. Sterling should be in any minute, and . . . ."

"Hey, Sterling's my brother, remember? What's he going to do kick me out? I'll just tell him I came over to see him and he wasn't here yet."

"But he'll know something is going on between us. We both left in the middle of the party Saturday. It will look suspicious."

"Actually, Sterling already confronted me about that." Robert said releasing her hand and sitting back.

"He did? What did he say?" Stacey asked uneasily.

"Oh he tried to warn me away from you. Lauren is concerned that something will happen to upset the wedding. I assured him that I had no intensions of ruining the wedding."

"But what did you say about us?" Stacey asked.

"I just told him we were seeing each other. A mutual arrangement." Robert said with a shrug.

"Oh." Stacey said with a sigh

"Wasn't I right?" Robert asked looking at her face.

"Yeah, you are right. It is a mutual decision. I just didn't want you to feel pressured into admitting anything more than what happened is going on."

Frowning at her agitated state Robert leaned over and grabbed her chin so she would look at his face.

"No one is making me do anything. I want to see you, you want to see me. I enjoy being with you, and as long as we decided to see each other it really isn't anyone else's business but ours. I like you Stacey, I like you a lot. I want to be with you. I know we just met, but when I look at you, when I touch you I feel something that I haven't felt for anyone. Tell me you don't feel it." Taking a deep breath he continued. "Tell me you don't feel it and I will walk away from this now."

"No. I do feel it." Stacey whispered looking at him with confusion in her eyes.

"Good." Robert said getting up from the chair and walking over to her. He pulled her up to him and kissed her.

Stacey enjoyed the slow, thorough kiss. She had never met anyone who kissed as well as Robert. Well, she corrected herself, Sterling had been a good kisser the one time they had kissed 6 years ago, but that didn't count. Robert was here and knew he was kissing her. He wanted to be kissing her. It was an intoxicating thought.

Robert pulled away from her lips but kept his hands on her waist. She swayed against him and slowly opened her eyes to look into his. He smiled at the glassy look in them, it made him feel powerful. Kissing her on the nose he let go of her and walked back to the kitchen. Maybe he needed to leave the physical contact to a more appropriate time and place, Robert thought to himself. He suddenly had an overpowering urge to take Stacey upstairs to her apartment and make love to her. Standing with his back to the doorway he took some deep breaths and steadied himself.

Stacey followed him into the kitchen and watched him as he took some breaths and stared out the back window. She thought she had been the only one affected by the kiss, but seeing him like this she knew she was wrong. Robert wanted her too, as much if not more than she wanted him. It was a heady thought. She decided to leave him alone for awhile to collect himself. It wasn't as if anything could happen now, so no need to inflame the situation.

She walked back to her desk just as Sterling walked in the front door. He was carrying his usual box of donuts. He stopped whistling however when he noticed Robert standing in the kitchen.

"Good morning Stacey." Sterling said nodding towards her.

"Good morning Sterling. Um Robert came by . . . . I um . . ."

"I came by to see Stacey." Robert replied turning from the window to face Sterling across the room.

"I see." Sterling said glaring at his brother.

"Do you see?" Robert said walking back to the reception area to stand beside Stacey's desk.

Oh boy, Stacey thought to herself. This was going to be uncomfortable no matter what was said. Sterling had the look of an over protective father, and Robert of a stubborn, rebellious son. She didn't want to be caught in this situation, but what could she do? Sterling didn't need to worry about them causing trouble with the wedding, but how could she tell him that?

"Yes, Robert and I met a few days ago, but never were introduced until your party Saturday. We hit it off, and are sort of seeing each other."

"So Robert has informed me." Sterling replied looking at her now.

"Be assured nothing that goes on between us will interfere with the wedding. We promise, don't we Robert?" Stacey said hitting Robert with her shoulder.

"Yeah, I told you yesterday that nothing would cause trouble for the wedding." Robert said peevishly.

"Fine, as long as I go on record for saying that you two better make sure it doesn't. If anything, I mean anything makes Lauren and my wedding day a disaster, I will personally hunt you down and make your lives a living hell."

With those words, Sterling walked down the hall to his office, shutting the door firmly behind him. Stacey and Robert stood still for a moment and then let out a sigh of relief.

"Wow, is he wound tight or what?" Robert laughed.

Staccy giggled and said "Yeah, Lauren has him pretty stressed."

They both broke out in a fit of laughter and sat down to start in on the donuts. Being a courteous hostess, Stacey let Robert take the first one, and was disappointed when he took her usual. Sensing her disappointment, Robert broke it in half and gave it to her. Stacey beamed at him and they bit into their pieces at the same time.

"These are so good." Stacey said wiping the glaze from her lips with her tongue.

"Don't do that." Robert said with a groan.

Stacey looked up puzzled and then laughed at his tortured expression, "Sorry." She mumbled as she took another bite.

"Don't apologize; just don't torture me when you know I can't kiss you." Robert said finishing his donut and getting up.

"Are you leaving?" Stacey asked standing too.

"Yeah, I did my damage for the day. I just hope Sterling doesn't take it out on you when I leave."

"Don't worry about him. I know how to handle Sterling." Stacey said waving her hand in the air.

"So would you like to go out for dinner with me sometime this week?"

"Um, well I'd have to find a babysitter." Stacey said cautiously.

"Will it be difficult to find one? If it is, the kids can come too." Robert said hurriedly.

"Oh please, I don't think so." Stacey said rolling her eyes. Did he think she was crazy? One night with the kids at a restaurant and he would high tail it out of Johnson City faster than a cat with his tail on fire.

"It was just a suggestion." Robert mumbled not knowing how to take her statement.

"I can arrange it. I just have to ask my parents if they mind keeping them a little later."

"Well call me when you have a night set. I can give you my cell so you can call me any time." Robert proceeded to write the number on a piece of post it paper from her desk.

"Ok, I shouldn't take too long, maybe by tomorrow I will know."

"Whenever." Robert said walking to the door, "I'll see you later."

After Robert was gone, Stacey stood staring at the closed door wondering what had happened. He had left so quickly, had she done or said something to make him mad? She couldn't remember anything other than the licking of her lips and his comment. She shook herself and sat down. She couldn't spend every minute of her day analyzing their conversations to make sure she didn't scare him off. Isn't that why she told him it had to be casual? She didn't have time to be in a relationship. Casual and physical that was all it could be. Maybe she had to make sure he knew it too.

Robert walked quickly to his car before he changed his mind and went back inside to kiss her. He knew that it wouldn't go well if he did. His body was already throbbing with need. What was he doing to do? He wanted Stacey like a man in the desert wanted water. His every thought was of her. He had to get it together or this whole thing would become a disaster. She wanted casual, he would give her casual. He had to just get a better grip on his emotions before their date. Revving the car's engine he tore down the street and headed home. A cold shower was definitely in order.

The rest of the day was pretty boring considering the way the first part of it started. Stacey and Sterling didn't really talk much as he had meeting and clients throughout the day. When Stacey left at 5:00 Sterling was still in his office catching up on paperwork from the week before. She told him she was leaving and that she had locked the front door. He waved at her, but didn't look up from the computer screen. Stacey shrugged and went up the backstairs to her apartment. She needed to take a few things to her parent's house so she didn't leave right away.

At 5:30 she was stepping out of her doorway as Sterling drove past the driveway down the road. Getting into her car she drove the ½ mile to her parent's house. The kids were outside playing and Stacey was greeted with yells and hugs that made her fall to the ground. She laughed at their happiness to see her. Her mom was in the house doing the dinner dishes and her dad was sitting on the porch reading the paper. Nothing much has changed, she thought to herself. This was a routine her parents had developed while she was growing up. It felt good seeing it still existed.

"Hi Dad." Stacey said walking up the steps with the children still attached to her legs.

"Hi honey. How was work today?" Her father asked looking up from the paper.

"Fine. Sterling is pretty busy so I have a lot of paperwork to do."

"Work is good for you." Her father replied going back to the paper.

"I agree with you 100%. I just wish I could spend more time with the kids." Stacey said sitting down and cuddling the two kids in her lap.

"Sometimes we don't have that luxury. Did you feel neglected by me growing up?" Her father asked looking at her over the top of the paper.

"Of course not. You always were there when I needed you."

"Well, don't you think Evan and Julie realize that too? You do a good job with them. I'm proud of you."

Stacey's eyes filled with tears at her father's unexpected praise. Sometimes she felt like such a disappointment to them. It was good to know they didn't feel that way about her. The day she had told them about Julie she had been so afraid of their reaction. They had simply hugged her and promised to help her in any way they could. With Evan she had really expected to be disowned. Who was stupid enough to pick two losers to father her children? Apparently she was. They had simply hugged her again and offered their support. They were the best parent, and she truly hoped that someday she could be half the parents they were.

"Thanks Dad." Stacey whispered reaching over to squeeze his shoulder.

Her father smiled and squeezed her hand in return and then resumed reading the paper. Stacey got up and carried the children into the house. Her mom called a hello from the kitchen and Stacey sat the kids on their feet telling them to get their things ready. Stacey then walked into the kitchen.

"Hey Mom, how are you doing?" Stacey asked kissing her mom on the cheek.

"Doing fine honey how was your day?"

"Alright. Did the kids behave for you today?"

"Stacey you always ask that and I tell you they were fine. Don't you believe me?"

"I just find it hard to believe Mom."

"Well they were angels for me. Julie helped make supper with me and Evan played at the table until Julie set it for dinner. Evan even helped clear the table when we were done."

"Wow how do you do it? I can't even get them to help clean their rooms."

"Ah, but you are their Mother, you are supposed to have the difficult time with them." Her mother laughed.

"Are you and Dad free to watch the kids a little later sometime this week?" Stacey finally blurted out.

"Sure, when did you have in mind?"

"I don't really know." Stacey said fidgeting with napkins on the table.

"Do you have an appointment or something?"

"No, well, yes, well . . ." Stacey didn't know what to say. It wasn't really a date, it was just dinner.

"Stacey?" Her mother asked turning from the dishes to look at her quizzically.

"A friend asked me to have dinner with him, and I just told him I had to check with you first."

"A friend?" Her mother said with her eyebrows raised to show her surprise, "A male friend?"

"Yes." Stacey said looking at her Mom.

"Well sure, any time this week is good. How about Thursday, if it isn't too late in the week for you?"

"That's fine. I'll just call and confirm with him and let you know when it is set."

"Stacey . . ." Her mom started.

"Mom, he's just a friend. We just met a few days ago. Don't worry; I'm not going to get knocked up again."

"Stacey, you know that isn't what I worry about. I just worry about you getting hurt. Men tend to have a problem with women that have another man's child. You have two children by two different men."

"He knows all that Mom. I told you, we are just friends having dinner."

"Ok honey if you say so. Would you like the kids to spend the night? It wouldn't be a problem. I can take them to school in the morning and you can sleep in."

Stacey gave her mom a hug and kissed her cheek, "You're the best." She said as she left the kitchen to find the kids.

They were waiting in the living room watching TV. Stacey's Dad had come in from the porch and was watching cartoons with the kids. She quickly told him the plans for Thursday and he nodded his agreement to the arrangements. Stacey soon told the kids it was time to go and they hugged and kissed their grandparents as they said goodbye. Stacey let out a breath of relief as she got in the car. That hadn't been half as bad as she had imagined. Her only problem was that she felt bad about telling her Mom that Robert was just a friend. It was a lie, they weren't friends at all, they were just lovers.

CHAPTER 6

Thursday was a cloudy day with highs only in the high 50's. Stacey sat in the office staring out the window trying to imagine the evening to come. Sterling had been civil all week. He hadn't brought in donuts again, and the whistle was missing when he entered the door. Lauren had called her Tuesday night to talk about the wedding, and a few hints had been thrown in about her and Robert. Stacey had assured her repeatedly that nothing would ruin the wedding; she just hoped that she was telling the truth.

The week had dragged by as she waited for her next chance to see Robert. He hadn't stopped by once since Monday, and their call on Tuesday had been short and stilted. Maybe he was regretting having asked me out again, Stacey tortured herself. He had agreed to pick her up after work and they would go out of town for a bite at a restaurant she hadn't been to before. Robert had said it was a family style place so there was no need to dress up. Stacey had thought it was strange, but had agreed. The last thing she wanted to do after a long day was wear a dress and heels anyway.

She had opted to wear a pair of black jeans and a light pink satin shell with a matching crocheted sweater. She had bought a pair of black dress boots a few weeks ago and they went well with the outfit. She had her hair down, as she knew that was how Robert liked it, but had added a few colorful clips for effect. When 5:00 hit she ran up to the apartment to quickly reapply some make-up and spray some perfume over her body. She tossed her hair with her hands to make it look fuller and grabbed a leather jacket in case it grew chilly later.

Robert was outside waiting for her when she came back down. He looked gorgeous in a natural way. He had on some blue jeans that hugged his muscular thighs and made her mouth water. His shirt was a black dress shirt that was unbuttoned at the collar to reveal a few tendrils of hair on his chest. He was wearing black cowboy style boots and Stacey almost jumped in the air with excitement. She loved a man in cowboy boots. It was her biggest turn on.

Putting a smile of indifference on her face she walked towards him. He was leaning against his red car with those booted feet crossed at the ankles, arms folded across his fabulous chest. The wind was playing with his long hair and he reached out to keep it down.

Robert almost had to keep his eyes from popping out of his head. Stacey looked like a knock out with her tight black jeans and lacy sweater that revealed satiny pink fabric. She looked like every one of his teenage dreams come to life. Her hair was down, all smooth honey blond with sparkling clips hitting the sun as she walked towards him. Her boots made a clicking sound as she walked toward him. His heart caught the rhythm and started to pound in time with the clicking that brought her closer and closer to him. He watched her hips swing from side to side as she walked. *God,* he prayed, *let me make it through the night without making a fool of myself.*

"Hello." Stacey said as she got closer to him.

"Hi" Robert said casually holding out a hand to her.

Stacey placed her hand in his and felt the familiar sparks go through her arm. She tightened her hold so that she wouldn't jerk away. She wouldn't let him know how the mere touch of his hand set her on fire. Robert opened the door for her and helped her in the car. When she was situated he slammed the door and walked to his side. Once inside he turned to Stacey and looked at her again. He hadn't been dreaming, she was still beautiful.

"What's wrong?" Stacey asked turning to meet his stare.

"Nothing, I just can't believe how lucky I am to be here with you." Robert whispered touching her cheek with the back of his hand.

Stacey blushed at his compliment. She never knew that a man could be so romantic. Robert was like a Prince Charming come to life. Inadvertently she leaned into his touch and Robert groaned. This was going to be harder than he thought. If she kept responding to his touch they wouldn't even make it to dinner.

"I think I'm the luck one." Stacey said turning to place her hand on his chest. She really didn't think dinner was as important as being with Robert at that moment. "Why don't we skip dinner and stay here?" She whispered slipping a finger inside the hole of his shirt and stroking his bare flesh.

Robert swallowed past the lump of desire in his throat. He wanted so much to take her up on that offer. The touch was like lightning to his blood. He could already feel his body responding to her touch, and her invitation with acceptance. This wasn't going the way he had planned at all. He had to do something fast or he would lose his objectivity.

"As much as I would like to take you up on that invitation, I think we should stick with the dinner plans." Robert said capturing her hand and placing a kiss on its palm.

"Tired of me already?" Stacey joked as she turned back towards the front of the car and avoided his glance.

"Hardly!" Robert snorted as he started the car and flew down the street.

"So why are we going out of town for dinner?" Stacey asked as they left Johnson City town limits.

"I thought a change of scenery would help us relax more." Robert replied half telling the truth.

"Oh, yeah, it wouldn't be too good to run into Sterling or Lauren would it? They might not like seeing us together right now."

"I don't give a flying fig what they think!" Robert exploded, "I wanted us to have time away from our life and everything in Johnson City to get to know each other."

Stacey clamped her mouth shut. It seemed everything she said was the wrong thing tonight. Was it her or him? She wondered keeping her eyes glued to the windshield.

The evening wasn't going well at all. She just hoped dinner wasn't as big a disaster.

They arrived at the restaurant 10 minutes later. The car was filled with an uncomfortable silence. Nether spoke as he parked the car and they got out. He walked slightly ahead of her and opened the door for her to go in first. The hostess arrived and they were seated at a booth in the back and it was relatively quiet since it was a Thursday. The waitress arrived with some water and menus. She told them of the daily special and than disappeared to get their drinks.

Stacey stared at the menu not saying a word. She didn't even remember what she ordered to drink. She had just blurted out whatever she thought of at the time. It was so uncomfortable between them. She didn't know what to do or say to change it. What had she said to make Robert get so defensive?

The waitress returned and Robert ordered first, when the waitress turned to her, Stacey mumbled an apology and looked quickly through the pages. She settled on the chicken cordon bleu and some French fries. God, she prayed, make this evening end quickly.

When the waitress left, Robert stared at Stacey's bent head. He hadn't meant to yell in the car. It had been stupid of him to get so upset at her. He just wished she would stop worrying about his brother and Lauren and worry about their feelings. He liked her, and wanted her to like him.

"I'm sorry I snapped at you in the car. I just get so frustrated with the whole Sterling and Lauren drama. I mean it isn't up to them who we see, is it? Just because we are in the wedding why should they have a say on whom we chose to date? Anyway, I'm sorry." Robert said grabbing her folded hands and squeezing them.

Stacey smiled and looked at Robert across the table, "Apology accepted. Now accept mine for being stupid and caring what they think. You're right of course. They don't run our lives and have no say. I just didn't think before I spoke. This was a good idea. I do feel more relaxed, now that we are here."

Robert leaned over the table and kissed her on the forehead. Stacey looked disappointed when he pulled back, having hoped he would kiss her on the lips, but she shrugged her shoulders and they held hands until the food arrived. The rest of the dinner was a learning experience. Robert told Stacey about his childhood and schooling at the drama college. He talked about his few acting jobs in California and about his dreams for the future. Stacey talked about her kids and her dreams of being an independent consultant someday. They lingered over coffee and dessert, sharing a peanut butter pie that was rich and delicious.

It was after 9 when they finally left the restaurant. Robert drove back towards Johnson City this time at a slower rate of speed. He really dreaded leaving her at the door when they got home. The evening had been everything he had hoped for. Stacey had opened up to him and really revealed herself to him. It had been a wonderful date, although he knew she wouldn't call it that. She had still made it clear that they were just being casual. He could bid his time, make her feel comfortable with him and than drop the ultimatum at her after they had been together longer.

When they got to Stacey's apartment, Robert drove to the back of the driveway. He cut the engine and walked her to the door. She unlocked it and stepped inside. Robert didn't know what to say or do. Should he kiss her, or just shake her hand and say good night.

"I had a wonderful time tonight." Stacey said looking at him through the darkness that separated them.

"Me too. I'm glad we did this." Robert said putting his hands in his pockets and returning her gaze.

"Would you like to come up for a drink? It isn't too late."

Ball in your court, Robert thought to himself, how very clever of her to leave it up to him to decide their fate.

"I don't know." He hedged trying to see how far she would go to convince him to come upstairs with her.

"The kids are at my parents all night. You don't have to rush home if you don't want to." Stacey said flipping on the stairway light and starting up the stairs.

Was that a hint to follow her up? Robert wondered as she reached the top step and turned to look at him. She raised an eyebrow and waited for him to decide what to do. What would she do if he told her he had to leave? Would she pout and try to get him to stay, or would she shrug and say good night with no fuss? Robert was temped to find out, but than she did something he hadn't expected, she sighed.

It wasn't an impatient sigh, or a sigh of confusion, it was a sigh of desire. A sigh of want and need and everything he had been feeling since he left her apartment Sunday morning. Abandoning his plan to make her react, he bounded up the stairs two at a time and took her in his arms. They fell against the wall and kissed as if they had been away from each other for years, not just a few days.

Stacey sighed again into his mouth, than moaned as he caressed her breast through the satiny fabric of her shell. Robert unlocked the door to her apartment and steered her into the room. This time they didn't make it to her bedroom. They shed clothing on the living room floor and wrapping her legs around his waist Robert backed her against the wall and thrust into her waiting heat. It was fast and furious, but it was just what they both wanted. Stacey came by the third thrust, ripping her mouth from his she cried out in wonder of the sensation and raked her nails down his back. Robert came a few seconds later groaning in pleasure.

When they could think again, Robert carried Stacey into her bedroom and they lay together on the cool sheets as the fires within them fanned again. They touched and kissed, whispered and moaned as they learned how each other responded to the others touch. It was a night of wonder and discovery. A night that Robert secretly hoped would convince Stacey that they were meant to be more than casual lovers.

Robert woke up around 3 a.m. disoriented and sated. His first thought was, "Where am I?" His second thought was "What time is it?" He turned to the clock on the bedside table and read the time. It was still dark outside, but he knew he would have to leave soon. Stacey would have to get up early to go to work, and he didn't want to get caught leaving her apartment when Sterling arrived at work. Rolling back towards Stacey, he stared at her sleeping face. She was so peaceful when she slept. Her face lost some of the worry that was constantly around her eyes and mouth. He leaned over and kissed her forehead, rubbed her shoulder and got off the bed.

"Where are you going?" Stacey mumbled sleepily when he stood up.

"I figured I should get out of here before morning." Robert whispered slipping on his pants.

"Don't go." Stacey whined as she squint her eyes and sat up.

"It's better this way." Robert said sitting down and giving her a hug.

"Better for whom?" Stacey asked wrapping an arm around his neck and holding him tight.

"Everyone." Robert said giving her one last squeeze and stood up.

Stacey went to get up and walk him to the door, but Robert stayed her with his hand, "I can find my way out. I'll call you later."

With that he was gone. Stacey stared at her bedroom door and listened for the front door to close behind him, hoping he would change him mind and join her back in bed. The door lightly clicked and she flopped back down into the bed with a "humph". No matter what Robert said, his leaving wasn't best for her. She had only known him for a few days and already she was starting to think he was the best thing that ever happened to her.

Robert walked out of the apartment and slumped against the closed door. Walking away had been the hardest thing he had ever done. He knew that in order for his plan to work he had to make Stacey see they were meant to be more than just friends, but this was more difficult than he imagined. He wanted to go back inside, crawl back into bed, and hold her tight.

Steeling himself Robert pushed away from the door and walked down the stairs. He started his car and as quietly as he could drove down the street. No sense in waking the neighborhood up, he thought to himself. That definitely wouldn't help his case. He drove through the streets of Johnson City in a daze. This was his town, his heritage. All his life he had been told about how his ancestors had built this City into what it was today and that someday he too would have a role in its success. Until now he hadn't taken that seriously, but after meeting Stacey he did. He could see himself building a life here. His dreams of acting seemed like just that, dreams. Being with Stacey was his main focus now. Her happiness was his goal in life. All he had to do was convince her of that too.

It was about 5a.m. when Robert pulled up to his father's house and parked his car. He unlocked the door and walked to his room. His father wouldn't be up for another 3 hours so he had plenty of time to set his plan into action. First a quick shower and then some breakfast to get his mind going. Today was going to be the beginning of his new life.

CHAPTER 7

Stacey woke up feeling groggy and unhappy. Last night had gone well, too well for a casual dinner. She hadn't wanted to feel anything but lust for Robert. After last nights conversation she was sure that she was headed into trouble. Robert didn't seem to be helping matters with his kind and patient personality or his chivalrous charm. She felt like she had practically seduced him into her bed last night which was a switch from how her sex life usually went. Guys usually came to her bed more than willing, now she had to force them there with female wiles and simpering. It wasn't like her at all.

Walking to the bathroom, she pulled her robe off the door and went to take a shower to wake up. She really hadn't wanted Robert to leave this morning. She wanted a repeat of last Sunday where they had shared breakfast and laughs together. He was right about leaving before Sterling caught them together, but he had been the one to say that he didn't care what Sterling and Lauren thought of their relationship. Sighing with frustration Stacey let the warm spray wash away her worries. Now wasn't the time to get into a relationship, and Robert wasn't the right guy for her. Hadn't he said he wanted to have an acting career? She wasn't willing to leave Johnson City and follow him all over the country while he fulfilled his dream. She had too many responsibilities here to be that carefree.

Shutting off the shower, Stacey dried herself with the towel and walked naked to her dresser. She pulled out clean underwear and some black stockings. A plan was formulating in her head, but she had to figure out how to apply it. Maybe Robert wasn't the man she would someday settle down with, but for now he was the man she lusted after. Somehow she had to get him to realize that was all they could have together. With another sigh, Stacey walked to her closet and picked out her blue and black pantsuit and finished getting dressed. How do you seduce a man who wants a commitment? Very carefully, she thought to herself.

Robert, meanwhile, was trying to figure out a way to make Stacey realize that they were meant to have a future together. She was more than willing to contribute the sex and seduction part of their relationship, but not the relationship commitment part. How do you get a woman to want to commit to you? He had a plan, a devious plan that could possibly backfire and cause him to lose her altogether. It was worth the risk, however, in his mind to go through with it. Sometimes a woman needed a little nudge in the right direction. He walked over to the phone and made the call to put the plan into action. He just hoped that his friend would come through for him like she promised. It was all in the timing and time was something he didn't have a lot of.

"Hey, Alyssa, it's me Rob. Yeah it's been a long time. I have a gig for you. Something small and personal. Can you be in Johnson City by Saturday? Great, ok yeah I'll explain it to you when you get here. Thanks babe, see you Saturday."

"Now I only hope I can pull this off." Robert said to himself out loud.

"What are you up to now?" Seth said walking into the room.

"Hey Dad, nothing, just talking to myself." Robert said shrugging his shoulders

"You sounded pretty determined. Anything I can help you with?"

"Only if you can help me win the heart of the girl I want to marry."

Seth chuckled and patted Robert on the back, "My boy that is an area I try to stay out of."

"I know Dad." Robert said laughing with his father.

"Do I know this girl?"

"As a matter of fact you do. It's Stacey." Robert said walking towards the coffee pot on the kitchen counter.

"Stacey?" Seth said looking confused for a minute.

"From the real estate office." Robert said clarifying pouring his coffee.

"God Damn it Robert! What are you thinking of? That girl has too many responsibilities to be messing around with you and your plans."

"Dad, I don't want to mess up her life, I want to be a part of it. I think I love her." Robert said turning around and looking at his father.

"Love! What do you know about love? All of 21 and think you are in love with a girl you just met, what 6 days ago? Stacey's a good girl that has had a rotten life. You need to pick someone else to mess with." Seth yelled getting upset

"Dad! You are not listening to me. I love her. I want to marry her someday. You can't expect me to just ignore my feelings and walk away from her. I at least think I deserve the chance to prove to her that I can be everything she needs."

Seth humphed and turned away. Love indeed! If he only had the patience to sit down and tell his youngest about love. The boy had lived in a fictional world practically all of his life. His dream was to be an actor, but so far he was an unemployed one. How did he expect to support a wife and two children when he had no job?

Sensing his father thoughts Robert said "I can do this Dad. You need to have more faith in me than that. I know she needs someone to support her and the kids. It is time for me to get a job and grow up. I know until now I haven't earned your respect, but I will, you'll see."

"Robert," Seth said with a sigh, "I have no doubt that you are sincere about your feelings for Stacey. She's a great girl, a wonderful mother, but you don't know what you are getting into."

"You're right I don't. But at least I should have the chance to prove I can do it. No one is willing to give me the chance. She is so concerned with being disappointed again she has lowered her standards to a casual fling. She doesn't even want to let me prove I can be good for her. Well I will prove I can do it. First I have to show her that she has feelings for me. Feelings that involve more than just lust."

"How do you plan on doing that?" Seth asked sweeping the air with his arms.

"A little jealousy is always a good motivator." Robert said chuckling.

"Jealousy? Boy, what do you have up your sleeve?"

"Just wait and see." Robert said finishing his coffee and walking out of the room.

Sterling didn't want to be too early at work just in case he ran into his brother leaving Stacey apartment. It wasn't exactly how he wanted to start his morning. The whole arrangement didn't set well with him. In fact he smelled trouble coming his way. Lauren was still upset about the whole thing as well. She had made plans of telling Stacey how she felt today at lunch. He was just glad he wasn't going to be around to hear it until later.

Pulling up to the building he noticed that his brother's car wasn't anywhere around, a good sign. He got out and opened the front door cautiously. Stacey sat behind her desk holding her coffee cup absently and staring into space. Of all the years she had worked for him and his father he never knew of her to daydream, especially at 9 a.m.

"Good morning." Sterling said loudly as he shut the door.

"Oh, good morning." Stacey said putting her cup down a little too quickly and splattering the desk with the coffee.

"Damn it." She cursed jumping up to get some paper towels.

"Sorry if I scared you." Sterling said when she came back out to clean up the mess.

"No I was just deep in thought." Stacey replied dumping the paper towels into her trash can.

"How's everything?" Sterling asked looking around the room.

"Fine. How is Lauren doing?"

"Great, as I am sure she will tell you at lunch today."

"Thanks for reminding me about lunch, I almost forgot." Stacey muttered the second part to herself.

"Are you sure everything's ok?" Sterling asked looking at the purple smudges under her eyes.

"Yeah, just a little tired today."

"Oh." Sterling replied not wanting to continue the topic of last night's events. "If you need me I'll be in the office."

"Ok." Stacey replied as he walked away.

Safely in his office Sterling sat behind his desk and prayed that everything would go smoothly until after the wedding. He had waited 6 years for this day to come, and he didn't want anything to ruin it for him. If his brother had the sense God gave him he would cool this whole affair down before someone got hurt. Unfortunately sometimes his brother wasn't the rational type. Maybe another talk would be in order. This time a more brotherly talk, not a lecture. Yes, he would call Robert and ask to see him at lunch time, maybe than he could have some peace of mind.

The morning went by too quickly for Stacey. Normally a nice lunch with her friend would make the day go slow, but today she dreaded their time together. She already knew what Lauren would talk about, and was tired of discussing her life with everyone. Sterling had been barricaded in his office all day, not even coming out for coffee or a chat. Why was everyone getting so worked up over a casual affair? It wasn't like they lived in the 1800's where such behavior was unheard of? She had two children by two different fathers for God's sake it wasn't like she was committing some great sin by dating a man she had no intension in marrying.

At 11:30 Lauren pulled up outside the building and honked her horn. Stacey called to Sterling she was leaving and he muttered ok. She grabbed her purse and walked to the car. Lauren sat in her bright pink and blue jogging suit looking all fresh and glowing with impending motherhood.

"Hello." Lauren said as Stacey sat down.

"Hi, how are you feeling?"

"Great. I never knew I could feel this good considering the morning sickness."

Stacey laughed remembering the morning sickness she had had with Evan. It had been terrible. Sometimes she had just slept on the bathroom floor until morning. It hadn't been worth getting back up since she would be back in the bathroom 5 minutes later.

They agreed to lunch at the restaurant up by Lauren's office. Stacey was still amazed that Sterling hadn't mentioned to Lauren about moving into his office with him yet. She knew eventually it would happen, but when? Maybe she would broach the subject herself today just to keep the topic away from her as long as she could.

"How are things with Robert going?" Lauren said as soon as they sat down.

Ok, maybe I will have to be quicker next time, Stacey thought to herself as she took her menu in hand. "As good, as can be expected."

"Still just a casual fling?" Lauren asked looking over her menu.

"Yeah, just sex." Stacey said flippantly.

"Stacey!" Lauren hissed looking at her across the table.

"What? I was just being honest." Stacey said making her eyes look wide with fiend innocence.

"How can you be so, so . . . ?" Lauren couldn't think of the words for Stacey's attitude.

"Honest?" Stacey said sipping her water.

"I was going to say crude, but if you think its honesty, than fine we will use the word."

"It isn't crude to have sex with a guy you find attractive. I know as a fact that you and Sterling had a similar arrangement when you came back to town, what, a whole 4 months ago?"

Lauren blushed at the memory. She had in fact set up the arrangement with Sterling because she hadn't wanted to get hurt by him again. With that idea in her mind she suddenly saw what Stacey was doing. She was protecting herself from more hurt and rejection, and basically setting herself and Robert up for failure.

"I didn't say there was anything wrong with having a relationship based on sex with a guy you find attractive. My only thought was for, not only your feelings, but Robert's as well."

"What do you mean?" Stacey asked squirming in her seat uncomfortably.

"You know what I mean." Lauren said looking at her friend directly in the eye.

"Robert agreed with the arrangement." Stacey said defensively.

"Willingly, or under duress?" Lauren asked pointedly.

"I don't know what you mean." Stacey repeated.

"Yes you do. Did you ask him what he wanted? Did he have a choice whether to have a relationship with you or did you tell him this was how it was going to be?"

"I don't know." Stacey whispered after a long pause.

"You see Stacey, Sterling and I both willingly agreed to the arrangement we had. We both didn't want more, or didn't want to admit we wanted more. You took that away from Robert and forced him to accept the arrangement you determined to be beneficial to you, not him."

Stacey didn't like the way the conversation had turned. She had expected to be lectured about getting involved with Robert at all, not on the way she was conducting her relationship. Had she backed Robert into a corner? She knew from the way he had acted that first day that he had wanted to be with her, but had she missed his intentions so completely she hadn't realized it? Was Lauren right about making the arrangement beneficial to her and not Robert? Could he possibly want more from her than just a sexual relationship? Was that why he had been so cautious last night?

"I see I have you thinking." Lauren said nodding her head in approval.

"Yeah, you really threw me for a loop. Here I expected to be told to back off Robert, and you are telling me to become more involved. I just don't understand what you want."

"It isn't what I want that matters." Lauren said sadly, "It's what you want, you and Robert. As I sat here thinking about your behavior I realized that maybe this arrangement wasn't what either of you wanted. When Sterling and I realized we loved each other, neither of us wanted to say it. We pretended everything was fine, but it wasn't. You can go ahead and continue having this attitude that sex is fine, but somewhere inside you are slowly dying. You can't just pretend it doesn't exist if it does. I'm not saying that you and Robert are in love, but don't you think that you two should take the time and find out before just imposing this restriction on your relationship?"

"I've been so use to being disappointed for so long that I guess I just figured I would cut out the relationship part. Robert seems so young and carefree. I didn't want him to feel pressured to stay with me for the kids so I just took them out of the equation without considering that maybe he might want them in it. I should have had more faith in him or at least ask him what he wanted."

"I agree. What can it hurt to ask? If he is happy with what you have now, than forget what I said and keep going, but what if he isn't? You owe it to both of you to see if something is there. Maybe he could be the one."

Stacey laughed and glanced around the room. Her laughter died when she saw Robert standing at the entrance to the restaurant speaking with the Hostess. Lauren looked over to where Stacey was looking. She saw the look that passed between Robert and Stacey and knew that she wasn't wrong about her suspicions. Robert cared for Stacey and Stacey, whether she wanted to admit it or not, cared for Robert.

"Why don't we invite Robert to join us?" Lauren said standing up to wave him over.

Robert came over and hugged Lauren. Lauren pulled the chair on the end of the table out for him to sit. Stacey was speechless. When she had seen him standing there she had felt her heart skip a beat. Now it was all she could do to control her racing pulse.

"Hi." Robert said looking at Stacey.

"Hi yourself." Stacey said unable to come up with anything witty to say.

"We haven't ordered yet Robert so feel free to join us."

"Actually I was supposed to meet Sterling here for lunch. I must be early."

"Oh I didn't know you had plans with Sterling today." Lauren said confused.

"I didn't. He called me about 10 o'clock and asked if I could meet him. It was quite unexpected."

Lauren frowned and kept her mouth shut. She didn't want to even begin to know what Sterling was up to. She knew he had been concerned about Robert and Stacey seeing each other, but she had specifically told him she would handle it. Now it seemed that Sterling was taking matters into his own hands. That wouldn't do, especially now that she had straightened out things to the way she felt comfortable. She glanced up and saw Sterling's truck pull up outside the building. Excusing herself she made a beeline out the door to confront him before he messed everything up. She caught him as he was stepping out of the truck.

"Get back in." Lauren said opening the passenger door and slamming it shut.

Sterling frowned at her command but got back inside and shut the door.

"What are you doing?" Lauren demanded.

"What do you mean?" Sterling asked furrowing his brows in confusion.

"I mean with Robert? Why are you meeting him for lunch today?"

"I can't have lunch with my brother?" Sterling asked lifting his eyebrows up in mock surprise.

"You know what I mean. Did you intend on saying something to him about Stacey?"

"It had come to mind." Sterling said looking at the window behind her head.

"I told you I would handle it." Lauren said touching his face with her finger so he would look at her.

"I know, but I thought I could try again before you did anything."

Lauren signed and Sterling was surprised by the smile on her lips. She leaned across the seat and kissed him. Sterling was shocked. That wasn't what he expected when she demanded he get back in the truck. Pulling back he looked at her with confusion. She laughed as she took his hand in hers.

"I already fixed it." She said merrily.

"What! Already? You just got here about 10 minutes ago."

"I know, but after 2 minutes of talking I discovered the key to the puzzle."

Sterling was confused. Puzzle? Key? What was she talking about?

"Oh darling don't you see? We were working the wrong angle this whole time. Instead of breaking them up, we should have been encouraging them to be together."

"What!" Sterling said incredulously.

"Stacey is falling in love with Robert, and I suspect Robert is falling for Stacey as well. Stacey forced Robert into this ridiculous arrangement because she didn't want to get hurt again, only she was hurting because she realized too late she had feelings for Robert."

"I'm confused. You want them to be together? But I thought you didn't want them to be together so it wouldn't ruin the wedding?"

"That was when I thought Robert would hurt Stacey. Now I realize it is Stacey who is hurting Robert." Lauren said gaily.

"And that's ok with you? You want my brother to get hurt?" Sterling said shocked.

"Not at all honey. Don't you see? If they admit they want to be together, no one will get hurt."

"I'm afraid I don't understand." Sterling said shaking his head.

Lauren slowly explained what she had discovered through her conversation with Stacey and how Stacey was going to talk to Robert about the possibility of a relationship. Sterling nodded when he thought he was expected to, but still didn't understand his soon-to-be wife. One minute she is upset that the wedding is going to be ruined by a torrent of hurt feelings, the next she is encouraging those feelings to bloom. It made no sense to him.

"So you see, it will all work out for the best this way." Lauren was saying when he tuned back in.

"Whatever you say." Sterling responded.

"You don't think they have a chance together do you?" Lauren gasped in shock.

"Lauren I know my brother, he isn't able to live in the real world all the time. He thrives on drama and melodramatics. He will not be able to settle down with Stacey, no matter how much he might care for her."

"I think you are wrong Sterling Johnson. Love can change even the most fickle of characters." Lauren said haughtily.

"And what made you the authority on that?" Sterling asked wearily.

"You, my dear. Loving you has changed me in so many ways. Before I discovered our love for the second time, I was so against love as were you I recall. Now we are the ones that should be toting the benefits of love to everyone."

"Oh yeah?" Sterling asked grabbing Lauren by the arm and hauling her into his arms, "I'm all for toting the benefits of love." He whispered before his lips claimed hers in a consuming kiss.

When they finally ended the kiss Lauren's face was flushed with passion and Sterling had to clamp down his desire to take her home now and finish what they started. Lauren made an attempt to straighten her hair that had been messed up by his roaming fingers and zipped up her jogging suit that had somehow been pulled down to her stomach.

"You have very quick fingers." She said accusingly.

"Ah, but you love those fingers any other time." Sterling said winking at her.

Lauren laughed and they both got out of the truck to go inside to their waiting lunch companions. Lauren was smiling when they entered the restaurant. Her smile turned to a frown when she noticed the heated look that was coming from the people sitting at the table she had left with such hopes not 15 minutes before. What had happened while she and Sterling were talking?

Walking over to the occupants of the table Lauren sat down and tried to lighten the tension. Sterling sat down on the opposite side of Robert and ordered a sandwich when the waitress came around. Robert and Stacey sat silently as they ate their food.

"So what took you so long?" Robert asked Sterling as he sipped his water.

"Lauren and I were talking about a little wedding emergency in the truck." Sterling lied easily.

"Yes." Lauren broke in hastily, "The caterers were having a problem with one of the dishes we has ordered. We had to decide on something else."

"Right." Stacey snorted from across the table.

"Excuse me?" Lauren said innocently.

"You heard me. The only emergency I can think of is what to do with Robert and me at the wedding if we suddenly hate each other."

"Stacey I . . . ." Lauren began.

"Don't worry. Robert and I are fine with being talked about behind our backs. You don't have to worry though, does she Robert? We are still just friends so you don't have to think anything will happen to upset the wedding."

With that Stacey stood up and quickly left the restaurant. Lauren sat staring at where Stacey had been sitting with her mouth open. What had just happened? Stacey and she had just discussed it and everything had been fine. Narrowing her eyes Lauren turned to Robert who was looking down at his food.

"What did you say?" She hissed through clenched teeth.

Robert looked up and first glanced at Sterling who arched an eyebrow and then at Lauren who was breathing fire at him. How do you explain what happened to your lovers best friend?

"It's between Stacey and me." Robert finally said shrugging his shoulders.

"The hell it is." Lauren spat hitting the table with her open palm making the plates and silverware clatter.

"It was nothing, really. I just explained to her that one of my friends from California was going to be in town Saturday and that I wouldn't be spending time with her until my friend left town."

"Is this friend a woman by any chance?" Sterling asked lightly.

"Yes."

Lauren hissed air out between her clenched teeth and growled in her throat. She wanted to kill Robert. It was only the second time in her life she wanted to kill anyone, the first was his brother Sterling, but that had been a misunderstanding, this was real. Could men be so stupid and callous?

"Did you tell Stacey she was just a friend or was she an ex-girlfriend?" Sterling asked trying to get more information.

"I just mentioned that we had dated off and on over the years, but nothing had come of it. My friend called to say she would be coming through town for a few weeks and wanted to know if I was going to be free. I told her yes since I am currently not committed to anything, or anyone. That's it."

"Well I guess it sounds innocent enough so why did Stacey get so upset?" Sterling asked confused.

"I don't know. Maybe when I mentioned that she would be staying with me at father's house she didn't like the idea." Robert said innocently.

"Robert!" Sterling exploded, "Are you that stupid? You're letting an old girlfriend stay with you?"

"She's a friend!" Robert said angrily, "Where should she sleep? The hotel in the next town, or do you prefer the street? I'm not married, nor am I officially dating anyone. If I want a "friend" to stay over than my "lover" will just have to accept it. We have no say on what the other does. That was her choice." Robert said defensively.

"I am very disappointed in you Robert for your heartless actions, but you are right. Stacey decided that this was the arrangement she wanted. However, maybe you should have run this by her first to see how she felt about it, just so you were both on the same page." Lauren said feeling her anger disburse.

"Thank you for at least agreeing to something I said Lauren. I didn't want anyone to get upset." Robert lied, "I just was trying to help a friend I haven't seen in awhile."

"Don't worry. I'm sure Stacey will be alright after she has time to realize how silly she is being." Lauren said patting his leg.

Robert smiled and Sterling looked at him hard. Something wasn't right here, Sterling thought to himself. Robert said he cared for Stacey and wanted a relationship with her so why would he risk making her mad at him by allowing a "friend" to stay with him? Something was going on here, he just didn't know what yet, but he would find out.

They finished their meals and Lauren and Sterling left to go back to work. Robert lingered over his coffee to think about how the day's events had gone. It had been difficult to lie to Stacey about Alyssa. It was true they had dated a few times, and had in fact slept together a few times, but Alyssa and he soon discovered they were not suited to be together and had stayed just friends like he said. He had wanted to abandon the whole plan when he saw the hurt in Stacey's eyes when he said he couldn't see her for a while, but he had to play this out. He couldn't let her know how he felt until she relented and allowed them to have a real relationship. He just hoped she wouldn't shut him out completely and dismiss him forever.

CHAPTER 8

Stacey walked back to the office and shut herself into the bathroom so she could cry in peace. She didn't think anyone would follow her, but she didn't want anyone to see her lose control. Robert's words reverberated through her head over and over until she wanted to scream. In fact she did scream. Of all the callous and hurtful things anyone had ever done to her that had been the worst. She didn't want to stop and think why his actions had hurt her so much. She had been the one to set the limits on their relationship, so she should be able to feel comfortable with them seeing other people.

It didn't matter though, because she felt like she would die. Here she was 26 years old with two children from different fathers and she couldn't even handle a casual affair without having her heart broken. What was wrong with her? Did she just have "kick me" written on her head? She cried until her tears stopped coming and then she washed her face, reapplied her make-up, and took a steadying breath. Opening the door she was relieved to see that no one had followed her. At least she had some of her dignity in place.

Taking the out to lunch sign of the door Stacey sat down at her desk and busied herself with work. At least if she was busy she didn't have to think about Robert. A few minutes later Sterling came back from lunch. He looked at her for a few minutes and then walked back to his office and shut the door. Stacey was relieved that he didn't stop to talk or ask her if she was alright. She didn't want to talk to anyone right now.

When 5 o'clock came she was happy to call it a day. She would be busy the rest of the evening with the kids and she didn't want to be around people any more today. The kids were rowdy and demanded her full attention until 9 when they went to bed. Stacey was so exhausted from the lack of sleep the night before and her day that she fell into bed at 9:30 and didn't awaken until her alarm sounded at 6:00 the next morning.

Robert, however, wished that he could find sleep so easily. He felt like he had really messed up with Stacey earlier at lunch. Instead of making her jealous, he seemed to have made her mad. Her reaction totally took him by surprise and the made him regret his plan. It was too late though to change it now. Alyssa would be here tomorrow and he had to at least attempt to make Stacey see they were meant to be together. He knew that his plan could spell disaster, but he had hoped that is would work out for the best.

After turning for the 100th time, Robert gave up on sleep and decided to watch television to clear his mind. Maybe some mindless talk show would make him forget his worries for the day. He turned on the TV and surfed through the channels looking for something to watch. At 3 a.m. he finally succumbed to his exhausted state and fell into a restless sleep. This dreams filled with Stacey and her reaction to his news about Alyssa. He was wake again by 5 when the phone beside his bed rang.

"Hello." He said irritably.

"Rob?" Alyssa said unsure if it was him from his gruff tone.

"Yes, Alyssa is that you? Where are you? Why are you calling to early?"

"I'm so sorry Rob. Something's come up and I can't come to New York. I was on my way to the airport last night and something stopped me. I can't explain it right now, but I just wanted to let you know before you headed out to meet me this morning."

"Are you ok?" Robert asked concerned.

"I'm fine, great in fact. I just can't give you the details right now, but I think I might have a part in a movie, a major part. I don't want to jinx it by saying anymore, but this could be the chance I've been waiting for."

"Hey that's great. Don't worry about not making it out. I think my plan wasn't laid out right anyway. Good luck with the movie. Let me know how it goes."

"I will, and sorry again for any problems I might have caused by not showing."

"Forget about it. Talk to you later."

"Bye Rob, good luck with whatever you are planning."

They hung up and Robert sighed with relief. Alyssa's not showing up could be the break he needed to make up with Stacey. If he somehow twisted it to make it sound like he had asked her not to come because he didn't want to ruin things with Stacey, she might forgive him and think of him as even more special. It was a thought. Smiling at his lucky turn of events Robert finally fell into a dreamless sleep.

Later that morning, Robert awoke to a loud banging on the door. It was after 11 according to the clock beside his bed, not as early as he had thought, but with the amount of sleep he had the night before it seemed a lot earlier. Rolling out of bed he walked to the bedroom door and opened it to stop whoever it was from pounding. He was surprised to find Stacey standing there. She seemed even more surprised to see him standing their naked except for a pair of boxers.

"Sorry to disturb you." She mumbled looking at his boxers.

"No need, come on in." Robert replied moving aside for her to enter his room.

Stacey seemed unsure as to whether to enter or not, but most have decided it was safe since his father was just down the stairs. The room was not anything like Stacey imagined his room being. It was actually neat, and clean. The bed was rumpled from his recent sleep, but other than that everything was put away and tidy. She liked the way the room was set up. It had a really nice flow that she imagined gave it's occupant a sense of peace and openness.

"I like your room." Stacey began looking around. "Did you decorate it yourself?"

"Actually no, it was like this when I moved back home last year. I have only added to its cluttered state since being here." Robert said sitting down on the bed.

"I see." Stacey said looking to see if there was anywhere safe to sit.

"You can sit next to me on the bed. I promise not to bite." Robert said smiling when he recognized her distress.

"I can stand." Stacey said not trusting herself to sit next to him.

"Whatever you prefer." Robert said looking at her across the room.

"I came here to apologize." Stacey began a little unsteadily.

"No need to apologize for anything." Robert said graciously.

"No, I feel like a fool after yesterday's scene at lunch. I really blew the whole thing out of proportion and I thought I should tell you that I was sorry."

"Stacey . . ." Robert began trying to stop her from her speech.

"Please Robert, let me finish. I have no right to tell you who you can and can't see. I was the one who put the restrictions on our relationship, as it was so nicely pointed out to me yesterday. It isn't fair to you for me to suddenly decide that we should change the terms of our relationship. If you want your "friend" to visit and stay here than that is fine. If you can't see me while she is here than I will just have to be content to see you after she is gone."

Stacey seemed to be stealing herself to continue. Robert felt that whatever she had to say must be really important to her for her to have come over here so early on a Saturday to talk to him.

"Robert," She began again walking across the room to be beside him, "I just want to be with you. If I have to share you with a hundred other woman I will. If you can only spare me a few minutes a week than that is enough for me. Whatever time you can give me, it is enough, because I want you in my life, in my bed. This is a lot more difficult than I imagined it being." Stacey said turning away.

Robert stood up and gently turned her to face him. Cupping her face in his hands he bent and gently kissed her parted lips. He wanted to convey his appreciation for her honesty, and a sense of his feelings in one kiss. It seemed to work. Stacey wrapped her arms around his waist and deepened the kiss. Robert was lost after that. His good intensions were thrown to the wind as he enfolded Stacey in his arms and kissed her with all the hunger he had inside of him. Stacey responded by moaning into his mouth words that he couldn't hear, but his heart understood.

Slowly Robert backed towards the bed bringing Stacey with him. He sat down and Stacey crawled onto his lap as they continued to kiss. Stacey's knit shirt was in Robert's way, so he lifted it over her head. She wasn't wearing a bra, was his first thought, his second was I'm lost. Sensing his thoughts, Stacey grinned and pushed Robert back onto the bed. Straddling his hips she leaned down and kissed his bare chest. She worked her way down to his boxers and then with a quick motion she was pulling them down his legs and throwing them to the floor.

"You're so beautiful." Stacey whispered staring at his naked form.

"Not as beautiful as you." Robert replied flipping her over onto her back and divesting her of the rest of her clothes.

Stacey sighed as Robert leaned down to suckle at her breasts. The feel of his mouth on her flesh was like nothing she had ever felt before. It gave her energy and strength while at the same time left her weak and supine. Her hands roamed his back and played with his thick silky hair. He moved lower down her torso and finally stopped at the apex of her thighs. Stacey knew what he was up to from last time and although it had been wonderful, she wanted him to be with her and feel the culmination of their passion together.

She tugged at his hair and he looked up at her with confusion. Stacey shook her head and understanding her needs Robert kissed his way back to her lips and spread her legs with his knee. His manhood probed her moist folds and finding her ready for him thrust into her waiting flesh. She arched with pleasure and her fingernails bite into his back sending Robert into a frenzy of need. Lifting up so he could better see her face, Robert gripped her buttocks and thrust deeper. Stacey cried out in wonder. Holding her tight against him he continued his thrusts until he felt her tighten around him. Letting go of her butt, he lowered onto her body and kissed her as she cried out in pleasure into his mouth. Moments later he stiffened and his moans of release mingled with hers as they continued to kiss and touch each other.

After a few minutes, Robert rolled to the side and gathered Stacey to him. She curled into him and they lay that way for several minutes enjoying the feeling of being held and caressed by each other. Eventually Stacey sat up and gave him a saucy grin.

"Does that mean you want me in your bed too?" Stacey asked ruffling his hair.

"There was never any doubt about that." Robert said grabbing her hand and kissing the palm.

"I was beginning to wonder." Stacey replied looking at his face.

"I always desired you Stacey, but my question has always been; will there ever be more to us than just that? I know you have your reasons for not wanting to get involved in a serious relationship, but I can't help but wonder if we are seriously underestimating our potential for more than what we have settled on."

"I'm sorry Robert." Stacey said looking at him sadly.

"Damn it Stacey stop being sorry. I just want you to know how I feel." Robert exploded getting out of the bed.

"I know, and I don't want you to keep wondering if we will ever be more than this."

"Stacey if this is all I can get, I will take it. As you said, I want you in my life as long and as much as you can give me. I'm just a greedy man and want more."

"Robert," Stacey began softly, "That is why I came over here. I've been thinking it over and part of what I was trying to say earlier was that I think we should consider changing our arrangement."

"What do you mean?" Robert asked holding his breath.

"I guess 1 was thinking we should start dating each other, exclusively."

Robert considered her words for a moment. Did she just way what he hoped she said? Had she really decided they should date? Letting out a whoop of delight, Robert picked Stacey up in his arms and hugged her tightly to him. She shrieked in startled delight as his enthusiasm. She was glad that he had taken to her comment with such joy. She just hoped that he wouldn't come to regret his decision when he met her kids.

"Um, the kids are downstairs with your father; do you think we should go down before someone comes up looking for us?" Stacey asked pulling slightly away from Robert's warm chest.

"You brought the kids here?" Robert asked looking at her with wonder.

"Well I thought if all went well than maybe we could all do something together, sort of a get to know you type deal." Stacey said shyly.

"That would be fantastic." Robert said hugging her again than setting her away from his so he could get out of bed.

Stacey was excited that he seemed happy. She watched from the bed as he went around the room gathering clothing from various parts of his dresser and closet. He started to dress and she wished that they could do this every day, like a real family. The very thought made her heart skip a beat and her breath catch in her throat. Could she really be seriously thinking about having a family with Robert? Just yesterday she didn't want anything to do with him because of his callous behavior, and today she was back in his bed and ready to settle down and have a normal family life with him. Was it possible she was in love with him? As if sensing her uneasiness, Robert turned and gave her a smile and thumbs up signal. She smiled back and let her thoughts rest. If it was love, than she was in serious trouble, but for today she was going to relax and enjoy her new relationship.

"Aren't you getting dressed?" Robert finally asked after he emerged from the bathroom ready to go downstairs.

"Yeah, I was just enjoying the peace and quiet while I can." Stacey sighed looking at the ceiling above his bed.

"Don't worry, with me around you are guaranteed to have more peace. I'll even take the kids out once in a while so you can have time alone."

"Promises, promises." Stacey laughed getting out of the bed and searching for her clothes on the floor.

Robert watched her get dressed and decided he liked the way the whole scene was laid out for him. He wanted to do this with her every day. Smiling at his thoughts he told himself to slow down, they were dating, exclusively, but not ready for the whole domestic thing. That was later down the road.

Once Stacey was dressed and had used his bathroom, they walked hand in hand down the hallway and down the stairs to the living room where the noise level indicated child activity. Robert grinned as he watched his father trying to draw a dog for Julie and tell a story to Evan at the same time. He couldn't help but be impressed.

"Having fun down here?" Robert finally asked setting off a storm of noise.

Julie nodded and watched Robert with wide eyes, while Evan screeched at the top of his lungs for his "mommy" and launched his compact body at Stacey's leg. Stacey let go of his hand to steady herself against the impact and let out a "whomf" as child collided with leg.

Robert bent down to look at Evan and introduced himself, "Hey Evan I'm Robert, a friend of your mommies." He said holding out his hand.

"Mommy!" Evan cried again as he buried his face in her leg and gripped even harder.

"Evan, stop being shy and say hello to Robert." Stacey said prying the child off of her leg and turning him to face Robert.

The child stuck his fingers in his mouth and stared at Robert with bright, watery eyes. Robert didn't want to upset the child anymore than he obviously was so he just ruffled his hair and turned his attention to his sister.

"Hi Julie, I'm Robert, nice to finally met you. Your mom has told me a lot about you." Robert said walking towards where Julie stood next to his father.

"Hi, are you Mr. Johnson's brother?" Julie asked looking at Robert with those bright blue eyes she must have inherited from her mother.

"Yeah I'm Sterling. I mean Mr. Johnson's brother." Robert said looking at Julie with a serious expression on his face.

"Oh ok than" Julie said in a small voice.

"So were you having a good time with my father? He isn't much of an artist, but he can do a good drawing of houses and trees." Robert said patting his father on the back.

"Yeah, lots of practice with those." Seth said grinning at Julie.

"Well I'm starving, is anyone else?" Robert said changing the subject.

"I'm hungry" Replied Stacey.

"Me too." Said Julie

"How about you Evan, are you hungry? I know a great place for waffles." Robert said turning back to Evan who was now in his mother's arms.

"Evan loves waffles." Julie replied excitedly.

"Great than let's all get ready and go than. Dad do you want to go with us?" Robert asked as he grabbed his keys off the table.

"No thanks I have to finish some business this morning before my golf game."

"Alright see you later than Dad."

"Thanks for watching the kids for me Mr. Johnson. You were a big help." Stacey said kissing his cheek.

"It was nothing. I enjoyed it and they are great kids." Seth said.

"Well let's go everyone." Robert called from the doorway.

Stacey walked out first carrying Evan and Julie followed behind her. Robert closed the door on his way out and told them they could take his car if they preferred. Stacey told him it was easier to just take hers and he shrugged and helped her buckle the kids into the car seats. She allowed him to drive since it was his idea to go out and he seemed to enjoy being behind the wheel. She was a little worried about his driving with the kids because she knew he was into speed, but he actually took his time and was relaxed.

They arrived at a side street café that Stacey usually didn't think about as being a breakfast place and was surprised to see so many vehicles lined up outside the building. Arching an eyebrow at Robert he grinned at her skepticism and helped get the kids out of the car. Inside the place was packed. Stacey had nightmares about places like this. Crowds and kids never got along, and she didn't want their first meal out together to be disaster.

"We can go somewhere else." Stacey said nervously.

"Nonsense, this will be fine." Robert said waving to the waitress walking past.

"Take a seat anywhere." The waitress said smiling at them on her way to a table.

"Came on." Robert said taking her hand in his and maneuvering around the room to the back.

They located a table in the corner away from most of the crowd and Stacey sighed in relief when she noticed crayons and a coloring book next to the table. She got one for both of the kids and picked up a menu that was on the table. Glancing at the prices next to the kid's selection Stacey felt her stomach drop to her feet. She would never be able to afford meals for both of the kids and herself.

"Breakfast is on me." Robert said looking at Stacey over the menu.

"Robert you don't have to do that." Stacey began.

"I invited you out so it is my responsibility to pay. Anyway, I want to do it. No arguments today Stacey." Robert said holding off her protests.

Sighing with consternation Stacey looked over the rest of the menu. Julie said she wanted waffles with strawberries and whipped cream and Evan broke in with is insistence that he too wanted that. Stacey knew it would be a waste of time getting them both a plate so she ordered one serving and two plates. The waitress gave her a rude grimace and asked if they wanted extra whipped cream. Stacey said no and went on to order coffee and milk for the drinks and a plate of toast for herself. Robert ordered the Belgium Waffles for himself as well with the extra whipped cream and a coffee. The waitress smiled at him and promised to be back shortly with their drinks.

"A friend of yours?" Stacey asked when the waitress was gone.

"Sort of." Robert said vaguely and went about helping Evan color his picture.

The drinks arrived promptly and Stacey couldn't help but see the wink the waitress gave Robert as she set down the coffee already made with sugar and creamer "the way you like it" she said as she ran her fingertips across his arm.

Robert said thank you and shifted slightly away from her touch. The waitress, Pamela, didn't seem to notice his stiff response and walked back to the front of the room.

Stacey stifled a giggle at his discomfort. Robert shot her a quelling look, but that made her laugh even more. The kids looked from their mom to Robert with wide eyes not knowing what they had missed. When she could control herself Stacey said sorry with a smile that said she wasn't really sorry at all. Robert kept looking at her with that look on his face, but his eyes were smiling.

"I thought you would be jealous or angry, not amused." Robert said reaching across the table and holding her hand in his.

"It is just too funny the way she is flirting so openly with you and you are trying to ward her off without being obvious."

"Maybe I just have to let her know I am taken and she will back off." Robert said caressing her hand.

"That might do the trick, but what else could she think when we walked in here together?" Stacey not convinced.

"Maybe she thinks you're my sister and kids, or a long lost cousin from out of town." Robert said looking at her across the table.

"You have a point, although I don't think she could mistake me for your sister, everyone in town knows the Johnson's only have two boys."

The food arrived with a flourish and Pamela had even gone to the trouble of having the waffle for the kids cut in half and placed on the plates so Stacey wouldn't have to hear them whining about sharing. Robert was given his food last. Pamela set it down slowly and with deliberation. Her breasts rubbed against his arm as she straightened up next to him. His face turned scarlet and he gripped his napkin in his lap.

"If you need anything else," She began looking at Robert alone, "don't be afraid to ask."

Stacey was about to burst out in another fit of giggles when Robert shot her another warning look. She excused herself to go to the bathroom to regain her composure and when she exited found Pamela waiting for her outside the door. Thinking the woman was waiting for the restroom, Stacey started to walk back to the table when her arm was captured by Pamela.

"What's the story with you and Robert?" She asked none too discreetly.

"Not that it's any of your business, but we are dating." Stacey said staring at the other woman directly.

"Since when?" Pamela asked snidely.

"This morning." Stacey said smiling at the memory of the events from this morning.

"Robert and I dated on and off a few years ago. I'll warn you that he isn't the type to settle down, especially with someone who has kids."

"Thanks for the warning, but Robert was actually the one who insisted on exclusive dating. I was just after his body." Stacey said the last to shock the woman, which it obviously did because her hand dropped from her arm and her mouth went to the floor.

Stacey walked to the table with a smirk on her face. That went well, she thought to herself. The kids had finished eating by the time she sat down and Robert was half way through his plate of waffles and extra whipped cream. Stacey ate her toast with enthusiasm with that smile on her face leaving Robert to wonder what she had done on the way back from the bathroom.

CHAPTER 9

The day went by in a dazed blur for Stacey. After breakfast they all went to the park to play. They had ice cream at the shop across the street and then lunch later at McDonalds. The kids were great, and enjoyed all of Robert's stories about his childhood growing up with Sterling. Stacey had to admit she enjoyed it too. It was nice to actually be able to relax and have someone else entertaining the kids.

By two o'clock Stacey realized that Evan was ready for a nap and told Robert that she would drop him off at home if he didn't need to go anywhere first. She hoped that if she got home soon enough the insuring tantrum would not happen before Robert got out of the car. Evan had already started to whine and complain about wanting more ice cream, but Robert had smiled and told him that maybe some other day they could have ice cream again.

Robert gave them each a kiss on the check before exiting the car and promised to see them soon. Julie was excited about the prospect and Evan grumbled about the ice cream again. Stacey smiled and told him she would call him later.

With a last wave she pulled out of the driveway and drove down the street to her apartment. It had been a perfect day to begin their new relationship. She couldn't have asked for a better day.

Her perfect day, however, came to a screeching halt as she pulled her car into the driveway of the apartment. Evan had fallen asleep in the back during the short ride across town and Julie was reading a book for school. The car parked across the street was her first clue that something was about to happen. Everyone knew the place was closed on Saturdays and the man sitting on the front steps looked like he had been there awhile.

Pulling the car into the garage, Stacey unstrapped the kids from their sets and carried Evan to the back door. She had Julie unlock the door and lock it after they all went inside. Stacey laid Evan in his bed and pulled off his shoes. She threw the afghan from the end of his bed over him and shut the door as she left.

"Julie, I'm going downstairs to see what that man wants. Don't open the door to anyone but me ok. You can never be too careful. I'll be right back." Stacey said walking down the stairs.

She unlocked the connecting door and locked it behind her. She didn't like the looks of the car and the man had a quality about him that look none to reassuring. Going to the front door she pulled it open and the man stood up and turned towards her. Stacey almost gasped in shock when she saw his face. The face she hadn't seen in over 3 years.

"What are you doing here?" She asked sharply.

"Stacey, you look great." The man said smiling hugely.

"I asked what you were doing here." Stacey repeated this time frowning at his happy expression.

"I was driving through town and remembered that we hooked up here a while back thought I would look you up and see how you were doing." The man said hopefully.

"I'm great now you can leave." Stacey said starting to shut the door in his face.

He was too quick and his hand pushed the door back open and his body filled the doorway blocking her from shutting it again. Eric stood in front of her looking like a man who was all too glad to see a woman. Stacey didn't doubt that he expected them to pick up where they had left off three years ago; after all she had been more than willing then. She, however, didn't want anything to do with him. Three years ago she had been young and full of misplaced rebellion. Three years ago she had been a single mother of 1 and ready to find some excitement that a traveling Carney could provide. He had been young, good looking, and ready for the challenge. Now she was in a new relationship with a man willing to take on her and her 2 children.

"Eric, please, I can't get involved with you. What we had was nice, but it was three years ago, I'm a different person now." Stacey said pleadingly.

"Honey don't act so put out." Eric said looking around the office. "I just wanted to say hi and see how you were doing, not cause you trouble."

"Well you being here could cause me trouble, big trouble. This is my employer's office and if he happened to find out I had a visitor here after hours I could get fired." Stacey lied trying to appeal to his sense of decency so that he would leave.

"Ah Stacey, Stacey, I wouldn't want to cause you any trouble. I just wanted to see you again, maybe pick up where we left off before my unfortunate incarceration." Eric joked making a grab for her.

"Don't touch me Eric." Stacey gritted through her teeth as she side stepped his touch.

"Oh playing hard to get are you. You always liked it a little rough didn't you baby." Eric said laughing as he grabbed for her again and he was able to manage to get her shirt in his fist.

"Please Eric, Julie is upstairs. I have to get back up there." Stacey pleaded looking at him with hopeful eyes.

"I almost forgot about Julie. How is that little sweetie doing? She must be big by now. She was just a little thing when I last saw her." Eric said with a goofy look on his facc.

"She's doing well. She started school this year." Stacey said remembering that Eric had always been good to Julie when she was around him.

"Great. Do you think I could just peek in to see her quick? I would like to see her just for a bit."

"No Eric, I don't think that is a good idea. She doesn't remember you; she was just 3 at the time. You would just confuse her." Stacey said trying not to panic.

"Alright." Eric said slowly. "I guess you're right. They don't remember much at that age."

"Right, so I really have to be going." Stacey said trying to pull away.

Before she could get anywhere, however, Eric jerked her to him and planted a rough kiss on her unsuspecting lips. She stood in shock as his mouth worked over hers. She had forgotten what a skilled kisser he was. His tongue shot out and traced her lips before he entered into her mouth and tangled with hers. When his hand found her breast and gave it a squeeze she was galvanized into action.

Tearing her lips from his she said angrily "What do you think you are doing?"

"Just saying hi to an old friend," Eric said grinning.

Stacey stepped out of his embrace and around her desk to place distance between them. She hadn't liked the fact that she had responded to his kiss. She had hoped that when she saw him again she would feel nothing but disgust, but she had liked his kiss. Feeling guilty and slightly dirty she shook herself and concentrated on getting him away from her son.

"Eric there isn't anything between us now. I am in a serious relationship and can't have you around messing that up. Please respect my wishes and leave."

"Sorry baby, I can't do that. I have a job in Johnson City starting Monday. I can't possibly walk away now."

"What! A job, where?" Stacey said aghast.

"Don't worry." Eric said smoothly, "It isn't here. It's for a construction company doing that condo project out by the park."

Stacey almost moaned in disbelief. He might not be working for Sterling directly, but he was working for the company that was doing the construction on Sterling's development. That could mean potential conversations involving Stacey or her kids. What would happen if Eric found out about Evan? Would he want to see him? Would he insist on shared custody or worse try to take him away? He was an ex-con would the courts really insist that he be able to have rights to his son? Stacey didn't want to think about it.

"Why stay around Johnson City? You never liked it here." Stacey said trying to get him to change him mind.

"I can't leave even if I wanted to. I'm on parole for 2 years. I have to stay here until that is over. Anyway, I think I have other reasons to stick around." Eric said eyeing Stacey.

"I'm not interested." Stacey said forcefully.

"Ah but I am." Eric said chuckling at her ire.

"Listen, Eric, I really have to get back upstairs. If you want to discuss this further, it will have to be at another time, and another place. You have to go."

"Alright, alright, I'm going. Calm down will you baby. I'll be in touch." Eric said walking out the door and to his car.

Stacey quickly shut and locked the front door before he came back. Leaning against the back of it she sighed in relief. He didn't know about Evan. *He will not find out about my son*, she promised herself. If she had to leave town for 2 years she wouldn't let Eric take her son from her.

Robert spent the rest of the day lounging around his father's house dreaming about the events of the day. It had been amazing. He could hardly believe that Stacey had finally came to him and said that she wanted to date him, exclusively. Just a few days before she wouldn't even label their time together as a date, and now they were in a committed relationship. Sighing with happiness, Robert watched television and imagined how great things would be once they finally settled into a routine.

He could picture Sunday dinners here, at his father's house, weeknights with occasional dinners at Stacey's place with bedtime book readings and kisses goodnight. For Saturday mornings he saw them going out as a family to the zoo or parks. Maybe dinners on Friday or Saturday nights with just Stacey and him while her parents or maybe Sterling and Lauren babysitting the kids. It was all such a perfect picture, that he felt a sense of peace and calm settle over him.

"What are you watching that cause that silly grin on your face?" Sterling asked breaking into Robert's dreamy thoughts.

"Oh, ah nothing, I was just thinking." Robert said startled.

"Yeah I could tell." Sterling replied turning the TV off and sitting on the couch next to Robert.

"What are you doing here?" Robert asked sitting up.

"Came over to talk to Dad, but I see he isn't home." Sterling said looking around the room.

"What are you looking for?" Robert asked watching Sterling glance around the room.

"Just wondering if my footloose and fancy-free brother was going to appear anytime soon," Sterling said half joking.

"Don't count on it." Robert replied, "I am a new man."

"Wow that is quite a statement coming from you. I never thought I would see the day." Sterling said play punching Robert in the arm.

"Well all I needed was the motivation of a good woman. She has totally changed my perspective on what is important in life. I mean, I know we just met, but I can see myself with Stacey."

"That's great Robert. I'm really happy for you." Sterling said sincerely.

"Good, because I wanted to ask you if you thought Lauren and you could baby-sit for us next weekend. I want to take Stacey away for a night just to let us get to know each other without the stresses of real life interfering."

"I'm sure something can be arranged. I will check with Lauren, but she is always looking for ways to brush up on our parenting skills. I'm sure she would see this as a good challenge."

"Alright, you check with Lauren and then I will ask Stacey. I'm sure she will love it, but sometimes she seems reluctant to leave the kids. Maybe someday I'll feel that way to."

"I don't think fathers ever have that problem." Sterling laughed standing up, "Tell Dad I came by to talk to him about the construction project. I need his opinion."

"Will do, I'll talk to you tomorrow at dinner."

"Sure. See you."

Sterling left and Robert resumed his dreaming. If all went well this weekend would be fantastic, just the thing Stacey and him needed to cement their relationship. He just hoped everything fell into place.

Stacey was having a difficult time thinking of a reason to leave town. She didn't want to appear desperate, but that was how she felt. Eric's unexpected appearance really threw her off. Things had finally started to go well with Robert and she was confident that he would be fine with the knowledge that Evan's father was in town, but she couldn't allow Eric to enter her son's life. If she could somehow arrange for her family to leave for a few months that would help her to feel more confident. Maybe she could get Robert to leave town with her. Wasn't he the one that wanted to live in California

Laurie Clark

or New York City anyway? Maybe if she expressed her willingness to leave with him he would want to go.

Whatever she chose she had exactly 30 minutes to make up her mind. Robert was picking them all up at 5 for Sunday dinner at his father's house. Tonight had to be the night for her to express her need to leave. Julie was in her room getting dressed and Evan was sitting on the floor playing with his toys. It had been a good day just the three of them, and she hoped the children's behavior would continue to be good throughout the dinner tonight.

"Julie are you dressed yet?" Stacey asked hopefully.

"Almost." Julie yelled back.

"Robert will be here soon. I want to brush your hair before we leave." Stacey said impatiently.

"Just a minute," Julie said followed by a crash.

Stacey jumped up quickly and ran to Julie's room. She let out a gasp as she noticed that the whole contents of the closet now lay on the floor and Julie was standing beside it with a guilty look on her face.

"What did you do?" Stacey asked accusingly.

"I was trying to reach a book on the top shelf, so I climbed up the shelving and it all fell down." Julie said defiantly.

"I see." Stacey said flatly, "and how many times have I told you to not climb the shelving in your closet?"

"A few," Julie said softly looking at the mess on the floor.

"When we get home I want you to pick this mess up. We don't have time now. Get your shoes and then go to my room. I want to do your hair."

"Ok mom." Julie muttered sadly.

Stacey walked back to the living room and picked up Evan off the floor. She carried his protesting form into her room and sat him on the bed so that he was in eye shot while she did Julie's hair. She didn't dare leave him unattended for more than a few minutes at a time or he got into everything. It was the age, but sometimes she wished they would revert back to helpless babies that couldn't walk, talk, or crawl their way to trouble.

At two minutes to five, they clamored down the stairs and waited for Robert on the front porch. It was starting to drizzle and they stood under the overhang watching the lightning flash in the distance. By the end of the night they were in for a big storm. Hopefully it would hold off until after they arrived back home. Robert arrived at five on the dot and they hurried to the car before they could get soaked by the ever increasing rain. Robert helped to strap the children into the car seats that Stacey had brought along and then they took off down the road.

"How was everyone's day?" Robert asked while he drove.

"Great." Julie piped up from the backseat, "Until I knocked everything down in my closet."

"How did you do that?" Robert asked looking at Julie through the rearview mirror.

"I was climbing my shelving in the closet." She said quietly.

"Oh well I'm sure you know that it is dangerous to be climbing the shelve, right? I hope you picked up the mess."

"I have to do it when we get back home." Julie said

"Well I hope it doesn't take you too long." Robert said sympathetically.

"So what did you do today?" Stacey asked changing the subject.

"Not much. Sundays are for lounging around and relaxing."

Stacey rolled her eyes and gave a snide snort. Relaxing and lounging were two words that didn't fit into her life anymore. Weekends were usually about playing and refereeing two children into playing with each other while she caught up on the neglected housework. She couldn't wait until Robert found out how she spent her weekends.

Robert on the other hand had to hide his grin at her obvious dislike of his reference to how Sundays should be spent. He knew she had it rough, working all week and than being with the kids alone on the weekends, but he planned on changing that soon. All he had to do was convince her to let him move in with her and everything would go fine.

"So what's for dinner?" Stacey asked.

"You'll have to wait and see. Lauren and Sterling were in charge of dinner this week so I'll be surprised too. I heard that Lauren isn't much of a cook, but Sterling knows how to make quite a feast out of nothing, I guess it's the bachelor in him."

"Well Lauren has been too busy making a living for herself to have time to learn to cook." Stacey said a little harshly.

"I realize that and I'm not saying anything against her, I was just letting you know that we are taking our chances with dinner." Robert said soothingly.

"Sorry, I guess I took offense." Stacey apologized.

"No problem. Let's just agree that Lauren and Sterling will be good for each other and that they have finally found the missing link in their lives."

"Sounds good to me."

They arrived at the house and made a quick dash inside before they could get totally drenched from the storm. The house was warm and filled with a great scent of home cooked food. The kids ran to Seth and he was immediately involved in a game of checkers with Julie with Evan sitting beside him. Stacey left Robert to help Julie with her strategy and found Lauren and Sterling in the kitchen disagreeing on how to prepare the salad.

"Hi guys." She said drawing two startled expressions from them.

"Hi Stacey." Lauren said warmly as she walked over and gave her friend a hug.

"Hi." Sterling said with a wave of his wet hands.

"How is dinner coming?" Stacey asked after Lauren had returned to her salad.

"Almost ready. Just fixing up the salad and we are all set."

Stacey hid a smile when she saw the way Lauren bumped Sterling out of her way to finish the salad to her specifications. Sterling shrugged and went about checking on the status of the main course. She envied the ease that existed between them and hoped that she someday found that same compatibility with someone.

"So how are things going with the wedding?" Stacey asked swiping a cucumber from the cutting board.

"Great, almost set. Just a few more details with the catering and the flowers and we should be set." Lauren said smiling.

"Good. Are you getting nervous? It's only two months away."

"No nervous isn't the word I would use." Lauren said looking over at Sterling who was busy stirring a sauce on the stove.

"Excited?" Stacey said helpfully.

Lauren smiled and had a dreamy look in her eyes, "Oh yeah definitely excited, and content."

Stacey could understand how Lauren felt. In the 6 years she had been gone Stacey had always felt in her heart that Lauren and Sterling were meant to be together. Now that they finally were about to be united in matrimony it felt like the relationship had finally been settled.

"I'm so happy for you, both of you. I just can't believe how quickly everything has happened. You two getting back together and the baby being here at the end of the year; it just all happened so fast."

Lauren hugged Stacey and they both wiped the tears off of their checks and laughed at their silliness. The food was brought out to the table and everyone gathered around to smell the delicious scent of good food. Lauren sat next to Sterling with Seth at the head of the table. Robert was across from Sterling and Stacey was next to him across from Lauren. Evan and Julie sat at the end of the table together. Stacey helped dish out the children's food and they all settled into a quiet, comfortable flow of conversation about the wedding. Sterling mentioned about their "surprise" honeymoon and that the office would be closed for two weeks while they were gone. Stacey didn't mind the break in the least. He had asked her a month ago if it would be ok with her and she had said it was fine. Now she was happy about the arrangement and took it as a lead into her mentioning her trip out of town.

"On the subject of trips." Stacey began hesitantly, "I was thinking, Robert, about taking a trip myself those two weeks."

"Oh really? What did you have in mind?" Robert asked with a smile.

"I was hoping we could go to New York City." Stacey said encouragingly.

"New York City?" Robert said incredulously. "Why would you want to go there?"

"Well you said that you wanted to get into acting, and since New York City is the big place to be discovered, besides California, I thought maybe we would all go with you to help you get discovered."

Robert stared at her in confusion. Did she want him to leave her? Was this her hint to him that he should start looking for a way to occupy his time? Before today Stacey had never expressed any interest in going to New York City.

"I want to go to New York City too." Julie burst in happily.

"Me go." Evan burst in not wanting to be left out.

"We all get to go." Stacey said happily.

"Are you sure?" Robert said again.

"Perfectly," Stacey said with enthusiasm.

"Alright than. Give me a few days to make some calls and we can go after the wedding."

Stacey leaned over and gave him a big kiss on the lips. The kids giggled and the adults laughed good-naturedly. The conversation had been tense and mystifying to them, but not more so than to Robert. Stacey sudden need to get out of town was puzzling and the first chance he had to talk to her he was going to find out what was really going on.

The rest of dinner was light and full of laughter. Stacey offered to help Lauren clean up and the men all took the children outside to play while they talked about business. Lauren was getting big with the baby and needed to sit down half way through with the dishes. Stacey finished them by herself but kept the conversation flowing.

"So what's going on?" Lauren finally asked.

"What do you mean?" Stacey asked innocently.

"You know what I mean. Why the sudden urge to leave town? Did something happen?"

"If I tell you, you have to promise not to tell Robert." Stacey said in a whisper.

"You know I would." Lauren said huffily.

"Evan's Dad showed up at my doorstep yesterday."

"And?" Lauren asked encouragingly.

"He doesn't know about Evan. He went to prison before I told him about Evan. He plans on staying around for a while, and indicated his intense desire to pick things up where they left off. He tracked me down and cornered me in the office while the kids where upstairs. I can't let him know about Evan."

"My God Stacey did he . . . you know?"

"No I was able to escape his grabbing hands, but he did kiss me. Oh My God Lauren his kiss was incredible. I thought with the way I feel about Robert I wouldn't enjoy another man's kiss, but it made me remember why I fell into bed with him in the first place."

"It is understandable that you would have some feelings for him, he is the father of your son, but that doesn't mean you would just hop into bed with him again. Is that why you want to leave, so you don't feel tempted to sleep with him?"

"No, I know I wouldn't do that. I love Robert and wouldn't ever do that to him. I just don't want Eric to know about Evan. What if he wants custody of him? Evan doesn't even know this man. For God's sake the man was in prison for drugs."

"Stacey you can't run forever." Lauren said softly taking her friend's hand in hers and giving it a squeeze.

"I know. I just don't want to deal with it yet. I'm scared of losing my baby." Stacey said with a sob.

Lauren embraced Stacey as she cried. She didn't know what to say to her friend. Never having been in this situation before it was difficult for her to know what the right answer was.

"Why don't you tell Robert about Eric? Maybe he can help you come up with a solution." Lauren said gently.

"What if Robert doesn't want to deal with this? He's so young and has so much living to do. Why would he want to be tied down to an older woman with two kids?"

"Maybe because he loves her!" Robert said entering the kitchen.

"Robert!" Stacey gasped looking over Lauren's shoulder at him standing in the doorway.

"How much did you hear?" Stacey asked uneasily.

"Enough to know that we need to have a serious talk." Robert said grimly.

"I'll leave you two along." Lauren said giving Stacey an encouraging squeeze and walking out the back door.

Stacey looked at Robert across the room. He had his brawny arms crossed over his chest and his face was unreadable. She didn't know where to begin or what to tell him. It was so difficult to talk about her feelings. For so many years she had been alone to handle all that life threw at her, and now she has someone willing to help her and she didn't know how to deal with that. Maybe if he didn't look so unhappy this would be easier.

"So what do you want to know?" Stacey asked wringing her hands nervously.

"How about telling me about this Eric guy." Robert said walking towards the chair Lauren had recently vacated and sitting down.

"Ok that sounds fair." Stacey said taking the seat opposite of him.

"Who is he and why don't you want me to find out about him?" Robert asked with a defiant toss of his head.

"Eric is Evan's father. Eric was a carnival worker at the field days here a few years back. It was a time in my life I'm not too proud of. I was just starting to get back into the dating scene after having been away while I had Julie. I went to the field days and noticed this guy running the rides. He was handsome in that dangerous sort of way that enthralls all the young girls. He gave me a big knowing grin as I stepped onto the Ferris wheel and when I got off he gave me a pinch on the butt. I came back the next day and the next and each time he would pinch me or pat me or caress me as I exited the ride. By the end of the third day I had decided to give him a whirl. I mean I figured he couldn't be that bad of a guy and he seemed nice."

Robert nodded without saying anything as Stacey talked about this guy touching her. He wanted to tear the guy's hands off and beat his face to a bloody pulp. He knew the type of guy she was describing. He used to be one of them as a young student of acting. You find a pretty, lonely girl and you give her some attention until she feels so flattered because you picked her out of the crowd and she falls into bed with you. Use them and loss them was the expression in California.

"Well he invited me over to his trailer after I finally got the nerve to ask his name. I'm not too proud of what happened that night or for the next week. I can't say that I regret it, because than I wouldn't have my son, but I can say that I wished I had better judgment. He was sweet and easy to talk to, but I didn't really know anything about him other than his name and that he had worked full time with the carnival since he was about 17. I didn't even know how old he was or his last name. It didn't seem important at the time."

Stacey stopped and tried to ignore the embarrassment she felt at describing her sexual relationship with another man to Robert. He was so silent and still she didn't know what expect of him. This wasn't the usual joking and carefree man she had met a few months ago.

"Anyway," Stacey said hurrying on, "A week after we officially met, I got a knock on my door at 3 am from the police. Eric was arrested for drugs and they wanted to know what information I had about him. I told them I didn't know anything about Eric or drugs. I felt like such a slut when I had to tell them that Eric and I had just been having sex and that was it. We never went out together anywhere and I never knew much about him other than what he told me. I went to his trial and I cried when he was sentenced to 5-10 years. Not because I would miss him or anything, but because I was stupid enough to get involved with someone who would sell drugs."

Robert reached for her hand across the table and placed a kiss on the palm. Stacey smiled and took a deep breath to continue on. The worst was over, but more had to be said.

"A few weeks later I found out I was pregnant. I was shocked because we had used protection. I was on the pill since I had Julie and he used a condom, most of the time. I knew a time or two one wasn't used, but I figured the pill would prevent the pregnancy and I would just get tested for anything else afterward. He assured me that he was clean, but people always say that, especially me. I was in denial for several months about the whole thing. Eventually, however, I had to face the truth and that was tough. My parents were disappointed but as supportive as ever. By then I had started working for your Dad and lived over the agency so I was on my own this time. I never told Eric about the baby. I never talked to him after that day at the trial. He wrote me a few letters but I never wrote back. What could I say? I didn't want a drug dealer around my children, or me."

"So what has happened that you suddenly are thinking about him?" Robert asked gently.

"He showed up at the house yesterday." Stacey said hesitantly.

"What?" Robert said with shock and anger.

"I saw a man standing outside the building when I got home yesterday and I locked the kids upstairs and told Julie not to open for anyone and call the police if she heard anything strange. He came in the office and told me he was out on parole. He got a job at a construction company in town and would be here for several years. I don't want him to know about Evan. I'm afraid of what he might try to do if he does find out about him."

"What did he say to you while he was there?" Robert asked.

"He expressed his eagerness to pick up where we left off and wanted to come up to the apartment. I told him that

that wasn't going to happen. I told him that Julie was up there and that I didn't want her to be confused at meeting him. He did know about Julie. I told him I had a daughter when we were together before. He even met her a few times. He was always nice to her, but as I said I don't want a drug dealer around my kids, even an ex-drug dealer."

"So that was the reason for the sudden eagerness to leave town? You want to run from him? Why give him that much power over you? He's an ex-con no judge would give your son to him. We can work this out together, Stacey. I wouldn't ever let anything happen to your children." Robert said holding her hands tighter in his.

"Thanks Robert. I do know you would do everything in your power to help me, but I just can't stand the thought of my child being near him. I don't think Eric would do anything to Evan, but I have been the one to raise Evan for the last 3 years and the thought of Eric being able to take him, it just scares me."

Robert stood up and walked around the table. He kneeled in front of Stacey and took her face in his hands. "You have no reason to fear him Stacey. I will never let anything bad happen to you or your children. I love you and will take care of you to my dying day. Do you understand what I'm saying?"

"I think so." Stacey breathed as she threw her arms around Robert's neck and gave him a deep kiss.

The clearing of a throat was the next thing they heard. Stacey reluctantly released Robert's lips and looked over his shoulder at Seth standing in the doorway. Giving him a weak smile she released Robert and he stood up to face his dad. He pulled Stacey up in front of him and said happily, "Stacey and I are getting married."

Seth smiled and said "It's about time." Then he gave them both a huge hug and yelled for Sterling and Lauren to bring the kids in for dessert.

Stacey stood in shock at Robert's announcement. She hadn't been prepared for it and couldn't believe that he had told his father that. She turned and looked at Robert with questioning eyes.

He smiled and caressed her check, "Well you are saying yes aren't you?" He asked cockily.

Stacey took a deep breath and said weakly, "Yes" and Robert gave her another kiss on the lips as the kids came in and started clamoring for dessert.

CHAPTER 10

The days went by in a whirl of activity. The wedding was quickly approaching and Stacey was kept busy with the preparations as well as keeping Lauren calm and in good spirits. Sterling had finally asked Lauren to move into the office with him and they spent a week moving her meager office furniture into the vacant room across the hall from Sterling. Robert came around the office daily to surprise Stacey with lunch, flowers, or an occasional gift. She was so busy that she didn't mind the fact that they had become engaged practically overnight and no one had said a word about it since that Sunday dinner three weeks before.

Another thing Stacey was grateful for was the fact the Eric hadn't made any more surprise visits to the house. She had feared that he would not take no for an answer and would be at her door all week. She didn't have time to ponder that, however, because everyone needed her attention and she was more than willing to give it to them.

The kids were out of school for the summer and that meant Stacey had more difficulty keeping them entertained after she got home from work at night. Robert was a big help with that as well. He would pick them up around 4 and then watch them upstairs until she got out at 5. The kids loved Robert and enjoyed his company. He spent most nights making dinner for them and helping her put them to bed. He would than stay for a few hours and they would talk about the future or cuddle on the couch and watch a movie. Some night they would make love and to Stacey those were the best nights. Robert was so tender sometimes that she cried, than other times he was intense and relentless making her cry out in ecstasy over and over until he had had enough and took his own pleasure.

Life was good, or so Stacey thought. A week before the wedding things went bad, however. The wedding was all set. The dresses fitted, the cake ordered, the food ready, the hall and church set to go. Nothing could ruin the day for Lauren and Sterling, except that the Saturday before the big day Lauren went into pre-term labor.

Stacey was sitting at the breakfast table with the kids when the phone rang. Thinking it was Robert calling to make plans for the day she was seriously taken back when the voice on the other end of the phone was Sterling.

"What's wrong?" Stacey asked worriedly.

"Lauren has gone into labor. We're at the hospital now. She wanted to let you know."

"Is she ok? Is the baby ok?" Stacey asked upset for her friend.

"So far it looks ok. The doctors have her relaxing and hooked up to the monitors. He gave her a shot of something to stop the labor." Sterling said confused.

"Ok, do you want me to come over? I can get my parents to watch the kids."

"No, no don't do that. I don't think the doctor will let anyone in anyway. I just wanted to let you know, in case . . . ." Sterling trailed off not able to finish his thoughts.

"Of course. Is Robert there?" Stacey asked softly.

"Um, no, I tried calling but no one was home. Could you do it? I really want to get in and be with Lauren."

"Sure Sterling don't worry I'll call him and your dad and let them know. Call me if anything happens."

"I will. Thanks Stacey."

"Don't worry I'm sure everything will be fine Sterling. Give Lauren a big hug from me and the kids."

"Ok, bye."

The line went dead and Stacey stared at the phone in disbelief. Why did this have to happen now? Why were these terrible things happening to two such wonderful people? Stacey shook off her thoughts and dialed Robert's cell. It rang 5 times and went to voice mail. She left an urgent message telling him to call her back as soon as he got the message. Where could he be? He didn't say he had plans for this morning. She called Seth's house and no one answered there either. Maybe she should go over and make sure everything was ok.

"Come on kids we need to get dressed and go to Grandpa Seth's house." Stacey said clapping her hands and herding them into their bedrooms.

"Is something wrong mom?" Julie asked with large eyes.

"I don't know honey. Something has happened to Lauren and I can't get a hold of Robert or Seth. I'm just worried that's all."

"Ok," Julie said as she went in to get dressed.

15 minutes later no one had called her back so she ushered the children into the car and was backing out into the street when a car pulled up and blocked the driveway. Groaning in disgust Stacey got out of the car and was ready to give the driver a piece of her mind when she saw Eric's face behind the wheel.

Straightening her back Stacey knocked on the window and motioned for him to roll it down.

"I need to leave, move the car." She said none too nicely.

"Nice to see you again Baby." Eric grinned propping his arm on the window and crudely looking her up and down.

"I'm not joking I need to leave, there's an emergency."

"You know every time I see you lately there is an emergency and you can't talk to me, why is that?" Eric asked reaching out to touch her bare leg.

Stacey jerked back as if burned and scowled at him, "Eric, I don't have time for this! A friend is at the hospital and I need to find her soon to be father-in-law and brother-in-law and let them know about it."

Eric considered her for a moment than relented. Starting the car he moved it up so she could back out and Stacey sighed in relief. Her relief was short lived however, when he got out of his car and started walking towards her.

"What do you want now?" She asked stepping back to the car.

"If you need to be going than I'm coming with you. We need to talk." Eric said grimly.

"You are not getting in my car." Stacey said woodenly.

"The hell I'm not." Eric said as he marched around and yanked open the passenger side door.

Stacey gasped and ran after him. She grabbed his arm and tried to pull his hand off the doorknob. The force of her body hitting his made the door slam shut. Eric turned and wrapped a vise like arm around her body, holding her tight against him. Stacey tried to stay calm but she was too angry and afraid to contain the scream that came from her throat.

"Mommy" Stacey heard Julie and Evan shouting through the car window at her.

"You are scaring the kids." Stacey panted as she tried to wiggle out of his grip.

"You are scaring your kids with all your craziness." Eric retorted.

"Let me go." Stacey said looking him in the eye for the first time.

Eric studied her expression and saw the anger, pain, and fear in her face. He understood why she was angry, but didn't understand the other emotions. They had shared a special time together 3 years ago and he hadn't ever hurt her in any way so he didn't know why she feared him. It didn't make sense to him, but than it did. His eyes widened a fraction and his mouth opened a form an Oh. He read Stacey's horror at his realization and held her tighter against him.

"How many kids do you have?" He asked tightly.

"Two." Stacey whispered on a sob.

"How old is the little boy?" Eric asked grimly.

"He's 3." Stacey said looking him in the eye.

Eric watched the way her eyes pleaded with him to not make her answer another question. He didn't want to see the look, but he did. She knew she was caught. The game was up. Her fear and pain weren't because of him, but because of the secret she was trying to keep from him.

"Were you ever going to tell me?" He asked gruffly.

"No." Stacey said through clenched teeth.

"I had a right to know. He's my son and I had a right to know about him." Eric started to shake her.

"You have no rights!" Stacey screamed, "You were in prison, you had no rights to my son, and just because you are here now doesn't give you any rights now."

"Damn you!" Eric screamed at her as he raised his hand.

Just as Stacey was bracing for a blow, a fist shot out and landed on Eric's jaw. His eyes widened in surprise and his arm went lax around her as he fell to the ground. Stacey turned and cried out in relief as she saw Robert standing behind her. She threw her arms around him and cried as he rocked her and stroked her hair.

"It's ok, baby, I'll never let anyone hurt you." He whispered into her ear.

The kids by this time were getting hysterical. They had finally gotten the seatbelts undone and here hopping out of the car to make sure their mommy was ok.

"It's ok kids, mommy's ok." Stacey reassured them.

"Who is that man, mommy?" Julie asked looking at a knocked out Eric.

"That Julie is a story for another time." Stacey said taking the kids and hugging them to her.

"You guys go back into the apartment. I'll take care of him." Robert said grimly.

"Robert, don't hurt him ok. Just please make him go home. I'll get a hold of him when I'm ready to explain things to everyone."

"Are you sure Stacey?" Robert said hesitantly.

"Yeah, I'm sure." Stacey gave Robert a broken smile and walked the kids back upstairs.

Stacey spent the next hour pacing the floor of the apartment waiting for Robert to come back. She couldn't imagine what could be keeping him, and she was starting to worry that something happened to him while he was taking Eric home. Had Eric become belligerent and started to attack Robert? Had Robert done something to Eric instead of taking him home? Was Robert coming back? All her doubts were chased away, however, when she heard Robert calling to her from the door.

"Stacey open up." He said pounding on the door.

Stacey whipped open the door and threw herself into his open arms. He engulfed her in a massive hug and stroked her hair. Stacey sobbed quietly against his chest. She was so relieved that he had come back to her.

"I was so afraid, Robert, so afraid." She whispered as her lips connected with his.

They kissed hungrily and for a moment Robert forgot about Eric and the information he had gotten from him over the last hour. There was only Stacey, soft and pliant in his arms. Her wet sweet mouth fused to his as if she didn't ever want to let him go. This was why he had talked with Eric before coming back to check on her and the kids. He knew she would be angry at what he was going to tell her, but for just this moment her being in his arms was enough.

"Where are the kids?" He asked huskily as she leading him to the bedroom.

"Sleeping." She answered shutting the door behind them and throwing the bolt. She smiled at his look and said, "Just in case."

Robert sighed as Stacey slid back into his arms and they resumed their kiss. She pushed him back onto the bed and straddled his hips. His shirt was half unbuttoned and she slid her hands through the remaining buttons and tugged the tails from his jeans. Bending down she planted open mouthed kisses on his chest, trailing down to the top of his jeans. Her fingers released the belt and the catch of this jeans and her mouth continued its downward trek.

Robert tightened is arms around her waist as she proceeded to drive him crazy with her delicious tongue and wicked mouth. His body soon was covered with a film of sweat from his restraint and he jerked her body up and captured her lips in a soul stealing kiss. Stacey lifted as Robert proceeded to take her shorts and underwear off of her. Stroking her thighs he settled her down onto his throbbing manhood. Stacey arched back as she sheathed him inside her moist heat. She groaned in pleasure as he then proceeded to arch into her as she thrust and moved upon him. It wasn't long before her muscles tightened around his swollen flesh and she cried out in pleasure. She felt him tense under her and she jerked her hips against him to increase his pleasure. Seconds later he moaned as his seed gushed into her womanhood.

Robert rolled her next to him hugging her close to his side. They laid there quietly as their breathing returned to normal and their flesh cooled. Stacey stroked Roberts arm with her fingertips and he played with her hair. Soon Stacey glanced up at him and saw the troubled look on his face. Not wanting to spoil the moment, however, she just pretended not to notice and rolled off the bed and went into the bathroom to freshen up.

When she returned to the bedroom Robert had righted his clothing and was sitting on a chair across the room from the bed. Stacey sat on the rumpled bed and looked at Robert. Whatever was troubling him seemed to make him want to put space between them, it made her heart ache for them both.

"What's wrong Robert?" Stacey finally asked reaching out for his hand.

"We need to talk." Robert said bluntly taking her offered hand.

"I figured that from you reserved and guarded expression. What do we need to talk about? Did you hear about Lauren? Did something happen?"

"It isn't about Lauren. My Dad told me that she was stable and the contractions had stopped. They have to keep her a few days to make sure they don't start again."

"Yeah that is what they told me when I called the hospital while you were gone."

"We need to talk about Eric." Robert said dropping her hand and standing up to walk to the window.

"What about him? What did he tell you?" Stacey asked becoming agitated.

"We had a nice little talk while I was driving him to his apartment. Do you know who he is? Anything about him other than what you told me?"

Stacey didn't like the accusatory tone Robert was using with her. It was insulting and uncalled for in her opinion. She had been completely honest when she had talked about

Eric to Robert. She didn't know much about Eric other than what she had said, but Robert apparently assumed she was keeping something from him.

"I told you everything about Eric that I know. I don't appreciate the way you are interrogating me over this. What did he tell you that got you all upset?"

"Well let's start with the basics. Eric isn't just some carnival worker who works at the fairs touring around the country. He's an undercover agent for the FBI, his name is Eric Walker."

Stacey started to laugh at his statement. If that wasn't the biggest bunch of bull she had heard she didn't know what was. Eric an FBI agent, that was too funny. Stacey looked at Robert and noticed his scowling face and tried to compose herself. Taking a deep breath she smiled and said calmly, "He told you this?"

"As a matter of fact he did. That isn't all he said either."

"Wait, wait, wait. He told you this and you believe him? An ex-con drug dealer? You believe he is an undercover FBI agent?"

"Well at first I was skeptical, but he confirmed it. He called his superior and had him talk to me on the phone.

He had his badge, gun, and his credentials all there for me to see. He's the real thing Stacey."

"Robert anyone can fake those "credentials", or a badge. The person on the phone was probably some buddy of his from prison going along with his ruse."

"Stacey, I called the FBI headquarters myself after I left the apartment. He's legit. He has been working undercover for the last 5 years, but now he is off the job. That's why they could tell me about him. He cracked the drug cartel last year and he is now a plain clothes FBI agent."

"So what's he doing here in Johnson City? Why would they send him here if he wasn't undercover anymore? That doesn't make sense?"

"He came here to find you." Robert said softly.

Stacey was speechless. Could it be true? Was Eric really an FBI agent and not the drug dealing ex-con she had imagined him to be for so many years? Stacey didn't want to believe that what Eric told Robert was true. First it was just too convenient that he suddenly told Robert when he hadn't bothered to say a word of it to Stacey. Of course he had told her they needed to talk, but she had assumed it was a ruse to get into her bed again. Secondly if she did believe that he was who he claimed to be, what would happen with her son? A federal agent trying to win custody of her son was different than an ex-con. Thirdly, it was a relief to realize she hadn't had such poor judgment about men as she had believed for so many years.

Robert watched the mix of emotions run across Stacey's face. He saw the disbelief, the fear, and finally the relief. He didn't know what she was thinking, but he had a pretty good guess. His only question was where did that leave him? Would she dump him and resume her relationship with Eric? Would she realize that she had secretly loved Eric and now knowing he wasn't the drug dealer he had been made out to be in her eyes discover that love and run off with him?

"So what do I do now?" Stacey asked out loud.

"That depends on you, I guess." Robert said with a shrug.

"I mean, did he say he wanted to talk to me about this? Am I supposed to contact him? What did he say?"

"Um, well I told him you would contact him when you were ready to talk to him, like you told me to do. He said that was fine. I have his address and cell phone number and you can either go there or call and arrange a time and place to meet."

"Alright, I guess I can do that. I am just so stunned by this. What should I do? I'm so confused." Stacey went to Robert and she laid her head on his back, wrapping her arms around his waist.

Robert wrapped his hands over hers and gave them a reassuring squeeze. He understood her confusion and didn't want to add any more burdens to her shoulders. Turning around to face her he smiled kindly and touched her cheek.

"You will know what is right when the time comes to make the decision. There isn't any rush. I'm not going anywhere, and I will always be here for you. We're friends right? Always remember that, first we were friends."

With that he kissed her lips softly and giving her one last hug walked out of the room, and then out of the apartment. Stacey stared after him with tears in her eyes. She feared that whatever choice she made she would be losing something precious to her.

CHAPTER 11

Robert drove to the hospital in a daze. The events of today had potentially changed his future forever. The news that Eric was an FBI agent and not the drug dealer that Stacey had assumed was shocking. In one moment the life he had imagined had been swept out of the picture and replaced by uncertainty and doubt. Would Stacey realize her love for the father of her son? All these years she had made herself believe the worst of Eric so that she wouldn't have to think about him as being in her life, but had she only deluded herself into thinking she wanted nothing more to do with him because of his past? Now that the truth was exposed would she embrace her feelings and send Robert packing?

So many questions raced through his head, but no answers would be forthcoming until after Stacey talked to Eric. Right now he had to focus on helping Sterling and Lauren through their difficult time. He was relieved to hear that Lauren was doing better and that the baby was fine. The wedding was next Saturday and he hoped they would be able to continue as planned. Only after that could he give into his emotions and doubts.

When he arrived at Lauren's hospital room Robert knocked tentatively on the door. He could hear Sterling's gruff voice as he talked to Lauren, comforting her. He heard Lauren's answering voice soft and low.

"Come in." Lauren called when Robert remained in the hallway.

"Hey guys, how is everyone feeling?" Robert asked gently as he hugged his soon to be sister-in-law and patted Sterling on the back.

"Much better now." Lauren said with a quiet chuckle, "Now only if your brother would believe me and stop hovering like a mother hen."

"Hey that's a father's job, to hover and look out for the mother of his unborn baby." Sterling said defensively.

"So when are they releasing you from this place?" Robert asked trying to keep the conversation light.

"Tomorrow, at the earliest. I insisted that it be by Monday because I have the last fitting for the dress than." Lauren said in consternation.

"Hey no need to rush things." Sterling said, "I don't care if we have to wait another week or another month to get married, as long as you and the baby are safe."

"Sterling, I don't want to wait any longer! I don't care if I'm still in this hospital bed Saturday, we are getting married." Lauren exclaimed.

"Ok, ok, calm down you two. No need to upset anyone. If you can't get to the wedding, the wedding can come to you. But Sterling is right; you and the baby's health are what are important." Robert consoled.

"So where is Stacey?" Sterling asked looking around.

"She's at home. Something came up and she told me to come on ahead and make sure everything was ok. She told me she called, didn't she say anything?"

"She did mention that an emergency had occurred, but she didn't say anything specific." Lauren said pensively.

"She wanted to be here, but it wasn't possible, so here I am to stand in for her." Robert said graciously.

"Is she ok? Did something happen with the kids?" Lauren asked concerned for her friend.

"No the kids are fine, she is fine. I really thing Stacey should be the one to tell you what happened, not me, so please don't worry about it and accept that she will be here as soon as she can to visit."

Lauren and Sterling looked at each other with frowns and than shrugged. Whatever it was seemed to have put Robert on the defensive and they didn't want to upset him more than he already was. Lauren was sure Stacey would be by later to talk to her, so she put away her questions and visited with Robert until he said he had to leave an hour later.

"That was strange." Sterling said as Robert left the room.

"Yeah, really strange. I hope it isn't anything serious. They seemed so happy Friday at the office. I wonder what could have made Robert so pensive."

"I don't know, but I'm sure you will get it out of Stacey when she comes by." Sterling said with a grin.

"You bet I will!" Lauren said sharply than laughed. "She isn't leaving this room until I know what is going on."

"Well as long as you are so sure of yourself." Sterling laughed as he climbed back in the bed beside her.

Lauren cuddled up against his warm body and hugged him tight. She didn't want him to know how scared she was about losing this baby, but she knew that he sensed her fear. He tightened his arms around her as if trying to give her body the strength it needed to keep the baby safe. Feeling secure she drifted off to sleep and dreamed of their wedding day.

Stacey gazed at the door for a while after Robert left. She didn't know what to do about the unexpected news. Eric was an FBI agent, not a drug dealer as she had thought all of these years. How did this news effect her belief about not only herself, but also of keeping Evan a secret from Eric? Did she want Eric in Evan's life? Would Eric want to be in his son's life? Would Robert understand if she maintained a relationship with Eric? So many questions, and the only way she would know the answers was to talk to Eric.

Galvanized into action, Stacey grabbed the phone and dialed the number on the paper in her hand. She prayed for the answering service and not his voice. She didn't know if she could actually get the courage to speak to him right now. What will she say to him? How will he respond?

"Hello" His voice came through loud and clear.

"Um, Eric?" Stacey squeaked out of her constricted throat.

"Stacey, is that you?" Eric asked hopefully.

"Yes." Stacey replied in a whisper.

"I'm glad you called me. I was afraid you wouldn't ever call." Eric laughed weakly.

"Well I just, um, well I think we need to talk about Evan." Stacey said cautiously.

"Yes, I agree." Eric replied seriously.

"Do you want to come over here? I mean if you aren't busy. I just have to take them, the kids I mean, to my parent's house and we could talk."

"I was hoping you could come over here." He said hopefully.

"Sure, I guess, it isn't too far from my parent's place. I'll drop them off and come over."

"Ok, about a half hour than?"

"Sure, I'll see you then."

Stacey hung up the phone and leaned against the table for support. A half hour to prepare for the meeting. It seemed like forever, but then again not enough time at all. She had to get the kids in the car. She had to explain to her parents what was happening. Stacey knocked on Julie's door and went inside. Julie was sitting on the floor playing with her dolls. She looked up as Stacey entered the room.

"What's wrong mommy?" Julie asked seeing the tears in Stacey's eyes.

"Nothing honey. You and your brother need to go to Grandma and Grandpa's house for a little while."

"Are you going to work?"

"No I have to go talk to that man who was here earlier. Than I have to go to the hospital and visit Lauren. She had some trouble with the baby and she needs some cheering up."

"Can I go and cheer her up?"

"Not this time baby. Maybe tomorrow, ok?"

"Ok mommy. Evan is playing in his room. Do you want me to go get him ready?"

"Sure, that would be great honey. Just grab a few toys and I'll meet you in the living room."

Julie went to her brother's room and helped him grab some toys for their trip. Stacey went into her bedroom and changed into a pair of clean shorts and a tank top in matching mint green. She brushed her hair and tied it back with a scrunchy. Applying a light dusting of make-up she grabbed her sandals and headed for the living room.

The kids were quiet on the ride to their grandparent's house. Stacey's parents met her at the door with worried looks on their faces. She gave a brief explanation of what was going on and told them she would call when she got to the hospital. She also promised to give Lauren and Sterling a hug and kiss from them all.

She hugged the children goodbye and told them to behave for their grandparents. She was assured they would and she waved as she drove down the street. Stacey cranked the music and sang along to distract herself from the upcoming talk. This was worse than the time she told her parents that she was pregnant, again.

Her car pulled up to the cabin located on the side road about 5 miles out of town. It was set among the trees and she would have missed it if Robert hadn't told her what to look for. Stacey slowly stepped out of the car and stood for a moment looking around at the beautiful country setting to calm her nerves. She jumped about ten feet when the cabin door opened and Eric stepped into the doorway.

He looked deliciously rumpled and sexy. His shorts were ragged denim cut offs, and he wasn't wearing a shirt. His dark hair was all tousled and laid across his forehead in a way that reminded Stacey of how it looked after they made love. His chest was as smooth and muscled as she remembered it, and his arms were well honed and defined. Clearing her throat and steeling her nerves she made her way towards him.

Eric smiled as she got closer. He could see the determination in her stride and on her face. He could tell by the way her eyes lit with an inner fire that she wasn't immune to his masculine charm. He sure wasn't immune to her beauty. For the past 4 years he had been dreaming of seeing Stacey again. It had been a long time since a woman fired his blood the way she did. Holding out his hand he grabbed Stacey's as she stepped up the stairs and into his cabin.

"Welcome to my humble abode." Eric said as he gestured to the two room cabin.

"Thanks." Stacey said as she stepped away from him and looked around.

The place was spotless and surprisingly well decorated. She could tell by the pictures hanging from the wall that Eric had more sides to him than she had ever realized. There were throw rugs on the hardwood floors, frilly chintz curtains in the window, candles on the end tables, and fresh flowers in a vase on the kitchen table.

"Do you have a decorator?" Stacey asked sarcastically.

"Actually I did it all myself when I moved in." Eric replied gesturing for Stacey to sit down on the leather sofa.

Ignoring his request, Stacey chose the rocker by the door. Eric grinned at her move, but didn't say anything. He knew she had reservations about him, but he planned on dispelling them quickly.

"Would you like a drink? I have some wine chilling in the refrigerator or maybe a cold beer?"

"How about a glass of water?" Stacey said narrowing her eyes at him.

"I can manage that." Eric agreed as he walked to the kitchenette and opened the refrigerator door. He returned with 2 bottles of water and handed one to Stacey.

Stacey accepted it and took a long drink. Her throat was dry and scratchy. She needed all the moisture she could get to be able to get through this conversation.

Eric sat down on the sofa, spreading out to make himself comfortable. Casually he sipped from the water as he studied Stacey's face. She looked extremely nervous. He would have felt sorry for her if he wasn't trying to guilt her into sleeping with him.

"So I guess you want to know why I lied to you for all these years." Eric finally said matter-of-factly.

"That would be a start." Stacey retorted.

"I work for the FBI, or I did up until last year. I was on a special assignment, a drug cartel in the New York area. I had to infiltrate the ring and become a member. When I met you that summer I had already achieved that and was on my way to the big guys." Eric paused to take a sip of water and lean forward across the distance between them. "Meeting you was not in the plans"

"So you just sort of went with it and used me." Stacey said angrily.

"I don't think I used you. I think it was a mutual attraction that couldn't be denied." Eric said smoothly.

Stacey snorted and looked away. Back then she had been a lonely single mother looking for attention. Eric had more than given it. She didn't deny her part in the seduction, but he was the one working undercover. He shouldn't have promised her all that she wanted if he knew he couldn't deliver.

"Come on Stacey, you know you wanted me as much as I wanted you, why deny it?"

"I'm not denying anything Eric. I just feel that you used my vulnerability to get what you wanted, sex."

Eric stood up and shot her a heated look. This wasn't going how he had hoped. 4 years ago Stacey had been a hot, lusty girl willing to give and receive passion anywhere with just the slightest provocation. Now she was defensive and touchy. She was blaming him for their affair and trying to make what they shared ugly and one-sided.

"You seemed to have forgotten how it was between us." Eric said snidely.

"I haven't forgotten anything." Stacey shouted as she shot to her feet.

Eric's eyes widened as she stormed to the bedroom and ripped off her clothes in the doorway. What was her game? He wondered as his feet blindly followed her to the doorway. Grabbing her naked body in his arms his mouth slammed down on hers with violent need. Her arms wrapped around his neck and pulled him tightly against her. Tongues thrust and parried as they stayed locked in the heated embrace.

Stacey finally jerked back from him and looked into his eyes. "Is this what you remember?" She asked as she rubbed against his throbbing body.

"Yes" Eric said gruffly as he caressed her breasts.

"Is this what you want? You want to pick up where we left off 4 years ago? You want me hot and wet and willing anytime, anyplace? You want me to fuck you senseless every time we see each other? You want me to believe that everything will be wonderful and blindly follow you anywhere?"

Eric didn't really understand what she was saying because her hand was stroking his manhood as she spoke. He continued to squeeze and stroke her breast with one hand as he reached for her secret treasure hidden below. Stacey opened for his fingers and arched back her head in surrender. Eric bent down to suckle the breast he was teasing and Stacey let out a yell of pleasure as he thrust his finger into her womanhood. Eric set a wild pace as Stacey continued to stroke and fondle his manhood. Soon she was so feverish that she grabbed his head and mashed her lips to his as she came apart in his hands.

Eric smiled as he trapped her screams of pleasure into his mouth. When she was limp and replete he picked her up into his arms and carried her into the bedroom and sat her onto the bed. Grabbing a condom off the nightstand he slipped it on and thrust into her so deep her back arched off the bed. He groaned in surrender as her body caressed his hot manhood. Gripping her thighs he opened her further and pounded into her as she crested the peak again contacted around him causing him to join her in pleasure.

"Eric!" Stacey's voice came from far away. In a daze Eric shook his head and stared at Stacey sitting across the living room from him. It had been a dream. A wonderfully, exotic dream; but a dream. Stacey was still glaring at him in the rocking chair, and he was still sitting on the couch across from her.

"What?" Eric asked taking a gulp of water and wiping the sweat from his forehead.

"Did you hear a thing I said?" Stacey asked exasperatedly.

Love's Promise

"Of course I did." Eric replied sarcastically.

"Good than you know that it will never happen. I love Robert now, and what we had 4 years ago is over. I was a young, lonely girl than with no one to love. You were an attractive, sexy guy that showered me with the attention I needed. When you left I had to pick myself up again and make a life for me and the children. We are all at a good place now and you coming back into town isn't going to change that. I've moved on and it is time you did the same."

"What about my son? Can I get visitation? A chance to bond? He deserves to know he has a father."

"Of course he does. I wouldn't deny either of you that. When I thought you were an ex-con drug dealer it was different. I didn't want him to be around that type of environment. Now that I know the truth about you I will be more than happy to see to it that you and Evan develop a father/son bond."

"I'm glad you see it that way because I plan on staying in town. If I can't have you, than at least I can have my son." Eric replied with steel in his voice.

Stacey didn't like the way it sounded, but wasn't going to argue with Eric anymore about it now. She wouldn't deny Eric his fatherly rights, but she wasn't going to let him control her life, or her children's.

"Well I guess it is settled than." Stacey said standing up. "Guess I'll be going now."

"Stacey?" Eric said hesitantly.

"Yes?" Stacey said turning towards him.

"What do you think would have happened if I'd stayed in town? I mean if I hadn't been working a case and had been a regular Carney? Do you think we would have stayed together?"

Stacey thought for a minute and smiled. "No, I don't think we would have stayed together." She said seriously as she gave him a pat on the check and walked out the door.

"Stacey?" Eric yelled again as she got into the car.

Stacey turned and looked at him with her eyebrows raised in question.

"We had some good times didn't we?"

Laughing at his uncertainty, Stacey nodded her head and got in her car and left before he could ask anything else. She glanced back once as she rounded the corner and saw his cocky smile looking back at her. As much as she hated to admit it leaving him had been difficult. He was one sexy man, but her heart belonged to Robert, and she wasn't about to mess that up with one night of fabulous, mind blowing sex with a dangerous man. Smiling to herself Stacey cranked up the radio and raced back to town.

CHAPTER 12

Robert paced the apartment waiting for Stacey to get back. He had let himself in with the spare key she had given to him last week. He knew she was with Eric right this minute and it killed him to think of what could be happening between them right now. He wasn't stupid or naive. He knew that Eric wanted Stacey back. Robert could tell by the way the man's eyes lit up when he said her name. Being in love with Stacey, himself, he couldn't blame him, but damn he wanted to punch Eric in the nose for even knowing what it was like to hold Stacey in his arms, to know the sensation of her finding repletion in his arms.

Shaking his head he sat down and turned on the television. He needed to find something to take his mind off of the whole thing. He promised himself he would accept whatever decision Stacey made. If she chose to go back to Eric and try to make a family together he would bow down gracefully and let them go ahead. It would be difficult and he would have a broken heart, but he had to think of what was best for Stacey and the kids. This wasn't a time to be selfish.

When he heard the key turning in the lock, Robert bolted to his feet. Stacey walked in looking tired and resigned. Robert's heart dropped to his feet when he saw the expression on her face. If her look was any indication, than he knew he wasn't going to like to hear what happened.

"Robert!" Stacey said surprised when she looked up and saw him standing there.

"Hi, I hope you don't mind I let myself in. I wanted to see you when you got back."

"No, I don't mind. That's why I gave you the key." Stacey sighed as she flung her purse on the counter and plopped down on the kitchen chair.

"How did things go?" Robert asked hesitantly.

"Good, things went good." Stacey said shaking her head empathically.

"Ok, well that is good right?"

"Oh, yes it is good." Stacey said distractedly.

"Stacey what's wrong?" Robert asked kneeling beside her and taking her hand in his.

"I'm just so upset over what is happening to Lauren. I mean she is such a nice person. Why do these things happen to her? And Sterling! Such a wonderful, caring, human being, and to have almost lost a second child, what is wrong with nature?"

Robert inwardly sighed with relief at her outpouring. He had thought she was down because of what happened with Eric, but instead she was upset over Lauren and Sterling. It was a load off of this mind. He was so happy he hugged her tight and stroked her hair as she cried.

"It's ok baby. They will be ok, you'll see. Lauren is strong and she will keep this baby safe. We just all have to pray for her and it will be ok."

"Oh Robert, I'm just so upset about everything. I tried to be strong for them when I went to visit, but I ended up crying and making Lauren comfort me. What kind of friend am I? I can't even be with my friend when she needs me." Stacey wailed.

"Hey, Lauren understands that things are messed up right now. She wouldn't want you to pretend everything was ok for her sake. I'm sure it helped her feel better not having to think about her problems for a minute."

"It just was such a mess. I mean this whole thing is such a mess: first Eric coming back, than him being an FBI agent not a drug dealer, than Lauren and Sterling almost losing this baby. The only good thing I can count on is you."

Robert pulled back from Stacey and looked into her watery eyes. "You can count on me?" He asked amazed.

"Oh Robert, I love you so much. I've been a fool for so long. I think I've loved you since I talked to you in Julie's that first day. You're everything I've ever wanted and more. You were right all along, I mean, so what if you are younger than me? You have more wisdom packed in those 22 years than most men do in 40 years."

Robert smiled and kissed her lips. Everything he had ever wanted to hear was coming from her lips. He had to trap them into his mouth so he could savor them fully. Soon, however, kissing wasn't enough and he pulled her down into his lap on the floor so he could feel her warm, pliant body against his.

"I love you Robert." Stacey whispered against their lips.

"And I love you Stacey." Robert whispered back as he pulled her down to the floor with him.

Robert reverently removed each layer of Stacey's clothing and savored each exposed piece of her body. Soon Stacey was wreathing in ecstasy under his delicate exploration. Robert took his time and made sure that Stacey never again doubted how much he loved her, or how much wisdom he had.

"Please Robert, now, I need you know." Stacey moaned as he suckled at her breasts.

"Not yet, honey, not yet." Robert soothed as he placed his finger on her lips.

Stacey sucked his finger into her mouth and stroked it with her tongue. Robert's breath quickened at the erotic sight and picked up the pace of his loving. He quickly divested himself of his clothing and flipping Stacey over on top of his body. She sheathed his manhood into her hot folds and set a pace that left them both gasping and aching for fulfillment.

Stacey felt herself tightening as her release hit her and she arched her head back as she rode the storm of passion. When she was limp from her release, Robert rolled them over so he was on top and grasping her waist he held her up so he could enter her more deeply. Stacey could feel him so fully that she climaxed again as he continued to thrust and withdrawal. Not wanting him to delay his passion any longer, Stacey reached up to stroke his chest, his belly, and finally the place where there bodies joined together. She tightened her thighs around his waist and arched up as she stroked him with her fingers. Seconds later she felt him shutter and he arched back as he continued to thrust deep within her.

Robert collapsed beside Stacey on the floor trying to catch his breath. He had never experience anything quite as exhilarating as what he had just done with Stacey. All of the times before had been wonderful, but this time it had been earth shattering. Stacey cuddled up beside him and he engulfed her in his arms, pulling her tight against his body.

"Now that was unbelievable." Stacey said with a giggle.

"Hey, why are you laughing?" Robert said with mock anger.

"Because I can't believe how damn fabulous you are." Stacey said with a smirk.

"I think it was a combination of both of us." Robert said with a sappy grin.

"Yeah, you could be right. I'm pretty fabulous too." Stacey said with a cocky grin that ended with a shriek as Robert pinched her bare bottom.

Before she could retaliate, however, he stood up and ran to the bathroom. Stacey stood up slowly testing out the strength of her legs and walked to the closed door. Testing the handle she found it unlocked and opened the door. Robert was bent over the shower knobs adjusting the temperature. Stacey got a chance to stare at his well shaped butt as he concentrated on his chore.

"Can I join you?" She asked walking up behind him and caressing the butt in question.

"Only if you promise to behave. I don't think I can do that again anytime soon." Robert stated with a groan as she ran her hand over his thigh and to his manhood that obediently started to stand to attention.

"Oh, I think you can." Stacey whispered naughtily as she stepped around him and into the shower. Robert joined her and she proved to him that he could in fact do it again.

An hour later Stacey and Robert where at her parent's house picking up the kids. The kids were happy to see Robert, as were her parents. In the time they had been together, her parent's had taken a liking to Robert which surprised Stacey. In the past her parent's hadn't every warmed up to any of the men she had brought home, but thinking back on it, it wasn't surprising considering the men she did date back then.

"So Stacey tells us that you are staying around Johnson City? Something about a job with the local theater group?" Her mother asked.

"Yes, actually I just found out a few days ago that they were hiring and applied. It was so fortunate that they were hiring when they were. I feared I would have to drive to Albany every day until I could find something closer."

"Well we are glad you are staying around. Stacey found herself a good man this time." Her mother continued gushing.

"Mom!" Stacey said exasperatedly.

"Well it is true Stacey. You couldn't have found a better man than Robert. He is a treasure."

"That's what I keep trying to tell Stacey." Robert said with a grin as he patted her leg.

"Oh shut up all of you." Stacey said with mock fierceness.

Everyone laughed and they continued to talk for another half hour about Robert's plans for the theater. Stacey was impressed with his plans. She hadn't realized that Robert had put so much thought into his projects. It gave her hope for their future, and for his remaining in Johnson City for awhile.

Soon it was time to leave and Robert carried the children to the car and they all waved as they drove down the street. Stacey sighed contentedly beside Robert as he steered them effortlessly through town. At her apartment Robert carried a sleeping Julie while Stacey carried an equally sleeping Evan up the stairs and deposited them into bed. When they were done they met back in the living room.

"Well I guess I should be leaving now, it's pretty late." Robert said as he placed his hands in his pocket.

Stacey looked at Robert and held out her hand to him. He removed his from his pocket and placed it in hers. Stacey tugged him behind her into the bedroom. Robert widened his eyes in surprise at her gesture. She was letting him know that she didn't want him to leave. She was allowing him to stay with her all night with the children home. It was a big step in their relationship.

"Are you sure about this Stacey? I understand that you don't want to confuse the children with our relationship." Robert said softly.

"Thanks for your understanding Robert, but I think it's time the kids realized that you will be a more permanent fixture around here."

Robert was so happy at her words that he hugged her tight and kissed her lips softy to convey his happiness at her decision. They undressed quietly and got into bed together. Robert pulled the sheets over their naked bodies and pulled Stacey close. Kissing her forehead he whispered a soft "good night" and within seconds they were both asleep.

CHAPTER 13

The day of the wedding dawned bright and clear. Stacey sat at the dressing table with Lauren and helped her apply her make-up. It had been a hectic two weeks and yet a joyous time for Stacey and Robert. Lauren stopped having contractions and although they had to delay the wedding a week, much to Lauren's dismay, the day arrived with baby still in the womb and the mother joyously relieved that everything was ok. Robert was now living with Stacey and the children. He had started his job at the theater company and was having a wonderful time. Stacey and Eric had set up visitation arrangements for Evan, and although the first meeting had been strained and uncomfortable, there was always hope for the future.

"Are you sure I look ok?" Lauren asked for the hundredth time.

"You look beautiful." Stacey said reassuringly for the hundredth time.

"You're just saying that because as my maid of honor you have too." Lauren grinned.

"Not true." Stacey said looking at Lauren critically.

And it was true. Lauren looked radiant in the cream silk gown. The top dipped low and tight across her heavy breasts, but then flowed loosely from her waist to her ankles in rich waves. There were pearls sown into the fabric across the neckline and in the shape of roses across the bottom of the gown. Lauren's hair was done in a crown of ringlets around her forehead and the rest hung down to her shoulders giving her the look of a Venusian Goddess. The vale was done in fresh white roses and baby's-breath. She wore a strand of pearls around her throat, a gift from Seth that had belonged to his wife. To Stacey, Lauren looked amazing, considering she was 8 months pregnant.

"I just hope I look half as good as you do when I get married." Stacey sighed wistfully.

Lauren gasped and wiped her head around to look at Stacey's smiling face. "HE PROPOSED?" Lauren shrieked happily.

"Officially this morning, when we got out of the shower." Stacey said grinning.

"Oh my god, when were you going to tell me?" Lauren asked.

"I just did." Stacey said with mock confusion.

"You little minx. I can't believe it. You've been here for 2 hours and didn't say a word. Robert! Is Robert going to tell Sterling?"

"I don't know. I mean it all happened so fast. After I said yes and we kissed and everything it was time to go so we didn't really talk about it." Stacey said with a blush remembering how they had made love on the bathroom floor.

"Well you talk to that man and see what he plans to do. I don't know if I can hold it in until after the ceremony. I'm just so happy for you both." Lauren said giving Stacey a hug.

"Thanks, I knew you would be. If it wasn't for you and Sterling we never would have met. It was fate."

"I'm all for fate, with everything that has happened in my life, how couldn't I be. You just remember that he loves you and that will be enough to get you all through anything."

"I will remember that." Stacey said with a solemn nod.

Just then Lauren's father came in the room to tell them it was time to start the ceremony. Stacey smiled as he kissed

Lauren's cheek and told her how beautiful she looked. The tears in his eyes were all it took to start Stacey crying again. Lauren scolded them for deliberately ruining her makeup and delicately wiped at the tears in her own eyes.

Stacey opened the door that lead to the backyard and heard the strains of Mozart coming through the load speakers. Taking her queue she started down the aisle. As she reached the gazebo that held the minister, the anxious groom, and her future groom, Stacey gave Robert a secret smile and he returned it with a sly wink.

As she took her place on the steps, Stacey turned as the bridal song started to play. Everyone gasped with delight at the beautiful picture Lauren made walking down the aisle with her father. Stacey noticed the love in Sterling's eyes as he watched the woman he had loved for so long come towards him. She could appreciate this moment for what it was and felt relieve and joy for her friends that this day had finally arrived.

The ceremony was brief yet beautiful. There wasn't a dry eye in the gardens as the vows were recited and rings placed on fingers. Cheers went up when they kissed and fresh flowers were thrown as the bride and groom walked arm in arm down the aisle and to the house.

"You look amazing." Robert whispered to Stacey as they followed the bride and groom down the aisle.

"Thank you. You look quite handsome yourself." Stacey said as they reached the doorway.

"I can't wait to get you home and show you what seeing you in that dress does to me." Robert growled as he allowed her to enter before him.

Stacey giggled as she walked into the house, "Who says we have to wait until we get home?"

Robert's eyebrows shot up at that and then he smiled devilishly. Now that he thought about it, there was a bedroom upstairs that he could use, his old one that he lived in before moving in with Stacey and the kids. He would just have to see about getting her alone for a few minutes.

"Just you wait. I'm going to take you up on that." Robert said huskily as they continued to the living room where the reception line would form.

"I'll hold you too it." Stacey said coyly as they entered the room.

The next few hours went by quickly. In fact Robert didn't have much time to think about a secret rendezvous with Stacey because he was so busy talking to everyone and playing the best man. Stacey, he noted was equally busy attending to Lauren. After the cake was cut and the toasts done, Robert soon found his chance to break away. He walked towards Stacey purposely as she sat at a table laughing with some friends. He bent towards her and whispered into her ear, "Meet me upstairs in 5." Then he was gone.

Stacey's eyes followed him as he went out of the tent and towards the house. When he was out of sight she hastily excused herself and followed the path he had taken seconds before. Damn 5 minutes, she thought, she had been waiting over 2 hours for this.

Once inside Stacey looked around the house to make sure no one was around before quickly climbing the stairs. Once up there, however, she didn't know which way to go. Was he in the bathroom, a bedroom? A second later she heard movement from the room down the hall on the right and went to the door.

"Robert, are you in there?" Stacey whispered at the door.

Not hearing an answer, Stacey opened the door and stepped inside. She heard a squeal of surprise then a grunt as a man rolled off the bed and fell to the floor. Stacey's eyes widened first in shock, then in humor at having walked into such a scene.

"I'm so sorry." She whispered around a giggle then walked back outside the room and quietly shut the door behind her.

She heard a man curse and try to reassure the woman inside that it was ok. Then he heard the woman raise her voice in anger at the man for not having locked the door. Staccy just walked down the hallway to the other bedroom that she knew had to belong to Robert.

When she opened the door she found Robert sitting on the bed with a bottle of champagne in one hand and two glasses in the other.

"What took you so long?" He asked with a frown.

"I went to the wrong room." Stacey said with a smirk, "I'll tell you about that later."

Robert looked at her questioningly, but Stacey didn't want to talk about it right then. She had other things on her mind, and talking wasn't one of them. Using only one hand she moved her hand to the zipper in the back of her dress and slowly slid it down as she walked to the bed and stood before Robert.

"Yes we have other more important things to do right now." Robert agreed with her as he set down the champagne and glasses on the table.

"We do indeed." Stacey said breathlessly as she slid the dress down her shoulders, arms, and then down to her waist.

Robert watched as he bare breasts came into view. He hadn't known she wasn't wearing a bra and it excited him to know she was bare under her dress. He reached out to caress her breasts and let out a sigh as she slid the dress down her legs and to the floor. Indeed she was completely naked under the dress, he thought as she straddled his lap and pushed him back onto the bed.

His clothing was quickly shed and soon they were rolling around on his bed touching and kissing each other as if it had been months, not just hours since they had last made love. Robert loved how free Stacey was when she made love to him. She never hide how much he excited her or how she felt about his touch. That was one of the reasons he loved her so much and knew that he would never know anyone like her again.

Afterwards, they lay in an exhausted heap on his bed. Stacey idly traced patterns on his chest with her fingers as she tried to regain her breathe. Being with Robert like this made her realize how lucky she was. Never had she met anyone who could read her wants and desires so quickly and efficiently as Robert did. When they made love it was like they were connected in some way. She was happy that in a few months she could call him husband and know that he would be hers forever.

"So tell me about going to the wrong room." Robert said as he stroked her hair.

"Hmmm, well that is quite a story in itself. But what I found in that room is what is funny." Stacey said as she propped herself up on her elbow to look at Robert.

"What could you have found so funny?"

"Not what, but whom." Stacey said with a laugh.

"You are killing me with anticipation." Robert said as he reached down and patted her naked butt.

"Ok, ok, I thought you were in the room down the hall to the right. I heard a noise and thought it was you so I called out your name then opened to door. Let me assure you it definitely wasn't you in the room." Stacey said with a laugh.

"Woman, will you just tell me what you saw . . . or whom you saw." Robert growled in frustration.

"You need to learn some patience." Stacey scolded causing Robert to haul her up over his chest and then roll her to her back.

"Strong man tactics will not help you." Stacey giggled as he trapped her arms above her head and rubbed against her chest with his causing her to stop giggling and gasp out in pleasure.

"No but seduction will." Robert said hoarsely as he forgot all about what had happened in the other room and went about making Stacey regret teasing him.

An hour later they emerged from the bedroom with their clothing intact and hair combed as best they could. They walked arm and arm to the reception that was now just about over and found the children sitting quietly beside Stacey's parents. Just then Stacey heard a ting of a glass and looked to the head table where Sterling and Lauren stood with the microphone between them.

"Ladies and Gentleman we have an announcement we would like to make for you all. It has come to our attention that our maid of honor and best man have decided to take the leap and become husband and wife. Please hold up your glasses and make a toast to them for a life filled with love and happiness."

Everyone cheered and clapped causing Stacey and Robert to blush in embarrassment. They walked towards the microphone and hugged Lauren and Sterling and thanked everyone for their well wishes.

Soon it was time to go home. The children were exhausted, the bride and groom had taken off for the honeymoon, which was back at Lauren's apartment since the baby could be coming at any moment, and the guest had all left for home. Robert drove them all back to Stacey's place and helped unload the car.

"Ok kids time for baths and bed." Stacey said as they entered the apartment.

"Awww mom!" They both chorused together in protest.

"None of that you two, in the bathroom now." Stacey said firmly.

"Do you want me to do the baths?" Robert asked as Stacey went to the bedroom to change into something more comfortable.

"Thanks, but I got it." Stacey said with a smile of appreciation.

Robert smiled back as he watched her slip out of the dress and into a pair of sweats and a t-shirt. As she started to walk back towards the bathroom, he stood in her way and gave her a light kiss on the lips.

"What was that for?" Stacey asked in confusion.

"Just because I love you." Robert replied as he caressed her soft cheek.

"Well in that case." Stacey said as she reached up and kissed him back.

The kiss was quick, but sweet in its intensity. When it was over, Stacey walked past him and into the children's bathroom. Robert stood in the bedroom for several seconds savoring the memory of the kiss. Then with a smile of his own he changed out of his own formal clothing and into a comfortable pair of jeans and a shirt. It was too early for bed, but too late to get into any projects. Maybe it would just be a movie night.

Once the kids' bath was finished they each came out to give him a hug and kiss then it was off to the bedroom for a story then bed. Robert set up the living room with candle light, popcorn, drinks, and a selection of movies. When Stacey came out 30 minutes later she was surprised to see everything ready.

"Wow you work fast." Stacey said with awe.

"Well it's been a busy day so I figured we could sit and relax before bed." Robert said with a shrug.

"You're a mind reader." Stacey said with a sigh as she sat beside him on the couch to watch the movie he had placed in the machine.

An hour later she was being shaken awake. With heavy eyelids she popped open one eye and stared into an amused pair of blue eyes.

"I'm sorry, I feel asleep." Stacey said guiltily.

"Don't worry about it, you're exhausted. Come on, let's go to bed." Robert said as he took her hand and led her to the bedroom.

"What would I do without you?" Stacey said as she slipped off her clothing and slid between the cool sheets.

"Probably the same thing you have done the past 6 years, take care of everything yourself." Robert said kindly.

"Hmmm, but it's so nice having someone to help." Stacey yawned.

"Well you will have me here for a long, long time." Robert said gently as he gathered her into his arms and held her close.

With a satisfied grin on his face, Robert slipped off the sleep with visions of the many happy years they would have together. Life was good and he intended for it to stay that way.